Dain tossed her
a sleeping bag

"The lower bunk is yours, and there's a pair of
Leon's pajamas inside the bag. They're more
your size than mine would be."

Karen stood waiting for him to leave before
she changed. He finally shrugged and walked
away, saying, "I'll be back to turn out the lamp."

The pajamas fitted reasonably well. She was
fastening the buttons when Dain pushed open
the door, and she gasped, "I'm not ready!"

He came out of the shadow, smiling faintly.
"I can see that."

Not to save her life could Karen have backed
away as he came toward her. He was naked
above the waist. With a gasp she pulled away
as his hand reached for her, but he stopped
her by twining his fingers into her hair.

SAMANTHA HARVEY
is also the author of these
Harlequin Romances

Boy
with Kite

Samantha Harvey

Harlequin Books

TORONTO • NEW YORK • LOS ANGELES • LONDON
AMSTERDAM • PARIS • SYDNEY • HAMBURG
STOCKHOLM • ATHENS • TOKYO • MILAN

Original hardcover edition published in 1982
by Mills & Boon Limited

ISBN 0-373-02541-6

Harlequin Romance first edition April 1983

CHAPTER ONE

IF Karen Fallon had not been engulfed by her troubles, she might have avoided a collision with the lean, dark-haired man who strode across the airport lounge at Rockhampton.

But Karen was thousands of miles from her home in England, stranded on the north-east coast of Australia, utterly miserable, with all her dreams shattered. She certainly wasn't in any mood to be taking notice of what was going on around her.

So quite suddenly, without any warning at all, she stepped straight into the hurrying man's path.

The impact sent her reeling. She clutched at a chair for support, lost her grip, and landed in a heap on the floor.

Around her, a fluttering cloud of papers settled; official-looking papers, typed, numbered and neatly set out, but released from the folder that had held them, because of the way Karen and the man had cannoned into each other.

There were still a few papers in the air. They settled around Karen as she gazed blankly up at the man who bent over her. Lean-faced and bitter-mouthed, he glared down at her, watching the skelter of papers with eyes that blazed in anger.

'Damnation!'

He made it sound like the most forceful expletive that had ever been uttered.

Karen quivered. Her confidence had taken a few devastating knocks in the past twenty-four hours, since she had landed in Australia, but she still had a few fragments of dignity left to grasp at. She tilted her chin at the irate man in a semblance of defiance.

'You should be helping me up,' she announced, and he stared at her incredulously.

'Helping you——!'

He clamped his lips together, as if he might be holding back a flood of words. Then he reached out an arm and yanked her with brutal suddenness to her feet.

'You can stand, I presume?'

His voice was iron-hard, totally without sympathy. 'You haven't broken a leg?'

'No, I haven't. No thanks to you.'

Reaction was setting in, and Karen stole a quick look at the jumbled papers around her. They were certainly in a mess, many of them upside down, some fluttering under chairs, others creased and crumpled by her movements as she scrambled to her feet.

She reached down tentatively to collect the nearest pages and the man snapped, 'Don't touch anything!' So then she watched silently as he gathered up his papers and stowed them as tidily as he could into the leather folder, his expression growing bleaker with every crumpled sheet.

Karen knew she ought to apologise. The whole thing had been entirely her fault. Well, almost entirely. Perhaps he, too, had been walking with his head down, although it didn't seem likely. He didn't look like a man who spent his time daydreaming.

The lean body in its cream safari suit moved swiftly and decisively as he swept the last of the scattered papers together and straightened himself.

His eyes were the darkest Karen had ever seen, almost jet-black, and they were piercing-bright as he stared at her from under black winged eyebrows that gave his face a strangely exotic look.

He said at last, 'If you're all in one piece, Miss

Whoever-you-are, perhaps we could go our separate ways. And in future do you think you might manage to look where you're going? It could save a heap of trouble.'

Abruptly, Karen stifled her belated apologies. He wouldn't get a single one of them, no matter how guilty she felt.

She said stiffly, 'I had a bag—an Airways bag——' With an exclamation of impatience, the man turned and stared around him. A swift movement retrieved the bag from where Karen had dropped it as she tumbled.

He glanced at the label and his lips twisted. 'Great Keppel Island,' he commented. 'Are you quite sure they're ready for you out there?'

'Yes.'

Karen did her best to sound convinced. She wasn't sure they were ready for her at all. Nobody, it seemed, wanted her today.

Of course, he hadn't meant it that way; he'd meant, They'll need to be insured against disaster on the island if you're going out there.

He was being sarcastic, but Karen thought the words had an ominous ring. Maybe they weren't ready for her, at that. Maybe it was an idiotic thing for a young girl, thousands of miles from home and friends, to let herself be hustled off so blindly, trustingly, to an island she'd never heard of, to take care of an old lady she'd never seen, without knowing exactly what awaited her or how she would cope.

Sitting in the plane that morning, all the way from Cairns to Rockhampton, Karen had been trying desperately to shore up her shattered confidence. Now she felt daunted. She looked up at the lean dark man with his bitter mouth, and a shockwave of doubt did terrible things to her composure.

'No,' she admitted flatly, 'I don't know whether they're ready for me, but I'm going, just the same.'

She was whisking herself away when the long arm reached out and a hand fastened around her wrist, strong fingers curling over her own where she held the strap of the Airways bag. She felt the contact almost as a shock, the fingers gripping hers were so vigorous. This was the hold of a man accustomed to grasping; not a gentle touch.

She pulled away, but the stranger held on. 'Not so fast! Aren't you a tourist? You're not planning to do anything silly, are you, like sleeping out underneath the coconut palms?'

'No I'm not.'

'You have friends?' He sounded doubtful.

'No, I don't have friends, not on the island. I have a job, looking after an old lady who's been ill. It was—it was arranged for me.' Determinedly, Karen tried to release her fingers from his grip. 'I'm going to a cabin in a valley. Wappa—Wappa——'

She flicked a quick glance at the piece of paper she clutched in her free hand, but the word was complicated. She couldn't remember how Andrew had pronounced it when he had sent her on her way.

'Wapparaburra Haven.' The lean man had no trouble with the difficult syllables, evidently he was used to them, but Karen wasn't sure she would ever learn to pronounce such a complex word. Haven, she understood. A haven was just what she needed, now that she had made a fool of herself by pursuing a man halfway across the world only to find he didn't need her and had lost no time steering her off somewhere else as fast as he could . . .

A haven . . . Oh yes, that was exactly the place for a silly, trusting, naïve young girl.

She stared dolefully at the face bent down so close

and searchingly towards hers. Surely they were the blackest eyes nature had ever produced. Jet-coloured and deep-set, with shadows around them, as if the man had not slept last night.

That makes two of us, Karen thought, without sympathy. Two of us who didn't sleep last night.

The stranger's skin was a deep tan, but his cheeks were thin and hollowed, jawbone pushing hard against tight skin, as if he hadn't eaten enough, either, for a while. All skin and bones, her mother would have said, cluck-clucking with sympathy.

But this man was strong enough; the hand grasping hers showed no signs of letting go. He was looking hard at her, assessing her out of those shrewd, unfeeling dark eyes.

So look at me, she thought, look me over . . . Is my broken heart showing? That ought to make you laugh, if nothing else would.

Then suddenly, surprisingly, the tall man allowed his tightened lips to relax. He didn't smile. Oh no, that would have been too much. But the mouth softened a little, so that Karen discovered it was a surprisingly well-shaped mouth when it wasn't doing beartrap imitations. His voice when he spoke was actually quite reasonable.

'I shouldn't worry too much,' he advised softly. 'Yellow hair, golden eyes, and that little-girl-lost look—you should fit in very well on Great Keppel Island, if they don't already have a resident mermaid.'

Then abruptly he let her go and strode away. Karen noticed he carried the folder of papers tucked carefully under the crook of his elbow, held against his body as if he might have been protecting them from further disaster.

Little girl lost. Was that how she looked? Did it really show that much?

What would the stranger have said if she had confessed, 'Yes, I am as good as lost. I've just arrived in Australia because six months ago in England I got myself sweet-talked into believing a man named Andrew Pinnar, who said he couldn't live without me. So I gave up a trip to Canada with my friends and flew out here instead ... And what do you know? He doesn't love me at all, or need me. In fact, he couldn't wait to get rid of me.'

She gulped miserably, because the pain was still new, the humiliation stunning.

She must try not to think about it, to put it behind her. She sat on a lounge chair and concentrated instead on the job Andrew had arranged for her.

'I can get you the position easily,' he had urged, his mouth sullen. 'No nursing involved, or anything special like that. Just a bit of cooking and companionship. A few weeks' holiday, really, with pay. Why don't you do the old girl a favour, and yourself as well, so you can see a bit of the country while you're here? That's what you came for, isn't it?'

No, it wasn't what she had come for. But if Andrew had managed to convince himself already, then Karen wouldn't argue.

It seemed unbelievable that only yesterday she had travelled all the way from Brisbane to Cairns, darted for the nearest telephone, and dialled the number Andrew had given her six months ago in England.

She had said, 'Andrew, it's Karen. You asked me to come, and here I am,' and instead of the delighted reaction she expected there had been the swift hiss of indrawn breath, and then he had muttered faintly, 'Oh, my God!' and that had been the beginning—only the beginning—of her devastating humiliation.

And when she said through the trembling of her shock, 'I'm here in Australia. In Cairns, at a motel.

Where you told me to come. Don't you remember.'

He'd answered tersely, 'Well, stay there, and for heaven's sake don't make any more telephone calls, and don't talk to anybody. I'll see you as soon as I can.'

In that moment she'd realised the awful truth. Andrew didn't want her. She had embarrassed him by taking off after him, pursuing him all the way from England to Australia, instead of going to Canada with her friends.

He'd forgotten the idea was his, forgotten all his ardent protestations . . . 'It'll be forever till you come, Karen honey. I can't live without you. Promise you'll fly out as soon as you can. Swear to me.'

. . . But that had been six months ago, while Andrew was visiting friends in England. And this was now, and very different.

Yesterday afternoon Andrew had arrived at the motel in Cairns very quickly. Karen didn't know how far out from the city the sugar-cane farm was situated that he'd boasted about in England, but it must have been pretty close. Either that, or he'd travelled at breakneck speed to get to the motel before she did something that might further embarrass him.

She'd watched him storm into the entrance, his handsome face dark as thunder; and suddenly it seemed to her that she had become a small girl again, waiting to be punished for something she hadn't done, expecting a reprimand she didn't deserve for some misdemeanour she hadn't intended.

That had been the story of her childhood: her constant failure to please a demanding father who had wanted a son and received instead an easily-intimidated daughter.

But yesterday, as she watched Andrew stamping towards her, Karen had drawn a deep breath and steadied herself.

Surely she wasn't going to let another man undermine her confidence? She was daunted, yes; but she
was a child no longer. Now she was old enough to
handle things for herself, so she would handle this.

But when Andrew stood frowning at her with undisguised hostility, her resolution wavered.

'Whatever are you doing here?' he almost snarled.

'You asked me to come,' Karen had reminded him
quietly. 'You begged me——' and his glance slid away
from hers before he mumbled, 'Well, how was I to
know——'

Almost at once he followed up with, 'What happened
to your friends? What were their names, Melanie and
Linda?'

And when she said, 'They've gone to Canada,' he
threw her an oblique glance as if he might have asked,
'Why didn't you go, too?' and then thought better of
it.

Which was just as well really, because Karen didn't
think she could stand much more of Andrew pretending he didn't remember all the hours he'd spent urging
her to change her plans and come to Australia.

'I need you, Karen my lovely. You beautiful English
lily,' he'd murmured; and although Karen had never
thought of herself as an English lily or any other flower
before that night, she had known instantly that it was
the most beautiful and wondrous thing anyone had
ever said to her.

For the first time in her life she had considered her
yellow hair and amber eyes as something to be treas-
ured, rather than despised.

My beautiful English lily——

Her heart half-turned in anguish. That wasn't what
Andrew had mumbled yesterday afternoon as he
hustled her quickly back to her motel unit without even
asking whether she wanted to be taken somewhere to

dinner. Not that she could have eaten . . .

She thought wryly of the cup of tea she had made in her room last night and then discarded because her throat was stiff with stifled pain. She wasn't anybody's beautiful English lily now. She was Karen Fallon, who had made an idiot of herself, believing extravagant promises, romanticising a man's passing fancy into something fine and deep and true, so that she followed him halfway across the world to find he didn't want her.

And he didn't intend to have her hanging around, either, making him feel uncomfortable. He'd been quick to offer to lend her the return fare to England, and when she hesitated he produced this job, arranging for her to go off somewhere hundreds of miles away to care for an invalid woman.

Only once he had looked at her, taking in the silken curtain of hair that touched her shoulders, the enormous amber eyes, soft trembling mouth, and it seemed to Karen that he wavered.

Then he muttered, 'No, you can't come here and mess things up for me now,' and Karen knew it was all over.

If he had reached out a hand to touch her, or flung an arm around her shoulders, she would have shrunk from his touch as if he were the bearer of plague.

He was hateful, a cheat and a liar; and he must have no compassion for others at all if he could say the things he'd said to her and then forget them so quickly and totally that he could just stand there, staring at her with accusing eyes, as if he remembered making no promises at all.

He had left her last night with the memory of that look. And early this morning, when he called at the motel to drive her to Cairns airport, to catch the plane to Rockhampton, he was as remote as a stranger.

She had watched him walking towards her from the motel entrance, until he was so close she saw the texture of his skin, the sheen of morning sunlight on his sleek brown hair and across the shoulders of his brown jacket.

Andrew was velvet, all velvet—eyes and lips and perfect features. Karen's heart stirred with pain as she remembered.

It had seemed incredible to her that at Cairns airport, Andrew could so calmly produce her airline tickets, one to Rockhampton, a separate ticket to Great Keppel Island; that he could organise her luggage, hand her a page of scrawled instructions and say, 'That's it, then, Karen. Victor West will meet you on the airstrip at Great Keppel. It's his aunt you'll be looking after,' then turn to walk away as if theirs had been a casual encounter.

Reaching for bravado, she had managed to say, 'Maybe I'll enjoy it after all,' and Andrew mumbled, 'Of course you will'; but neither of them believed it.

Karen had been astonished at the control in her own voice. How calm it sounded, how emotionless. Her eyes met Andrew's uncomfortable glance without flinching. She went on coolly, 'I have traveller's cheques, enough to last until my first pay day.'

He flushed again and shuffled his feet uncomfortably, and said, 'Oh, for goodness' sake, Karen——'

Then his lips clamped in a stubborn line, and he walked away.

Andrew had almost reached the doorway when he paused and looked back, hesitating in mid-movement as though some inclination stronger than himself forced him to make this one last turn-around to look at the girl he was deserting.

Karen did not know that the morning sunlight

beamed in through a window, turning the pale yellow of her straight hair to shimmering white-gold, and her eyes were wide and gold and desolate, yet quaintly dignified. She only knew that he stood staring at her, grim-faced and irresolute, until he shrugged those elegant shoulders and strode away.

She had watched him leave, knowing that she had never been so alone and insecure in all the nineteen years of her life.

And she didn't feel much better now, an hour later, gathering together her shattered dignity after her unfortunate encounter with the dark man. Her control was only superficial.

She sat waiting for the second part of her flight to Great Keppel Island, and when it was announced she picked up her Airways bag with trembling fingers and walked out to where the bush pilot's plane waited on the runway.

Half dazed, she boarded, fingers still unsteady as she fumbled with her seat-belt.

There were seventeen passengers on the plane for Great Keppel Island. The seventeenth was a lean dark man who boarded at the last minute, carefully holding his folder of papers under one arm. Karen stared at him indignantly. He hadn't mentioned anything about flying out to the island. Come to think of it, he had been extremely secretive.

He settled himself in a seat not far from her, arranging the folder of papers on his lap as he fastened his seat-belt, not looking at anybody.

As the plane took off, Karen glanced down at the coastline, then at the blue-green ocean with its scattered islands, ignoring the man in front of her.

Twenty minutes later, the small plane glided down on to an airstrip on the largest island of them all. A smiling girl in a flower-patterned sundress greeted each alighting passenger with a hibiscus flower.

'Welcome.' Her voice was warm, honey-sweet. Karen looked down at the flower in her hand, petals of palest pink with scarlet threads running from a deep-red throat, the flower lying on her palm like a piece of captured perfection.

She lifted her head and saw for the first time that the sky was blazing blue; that sunlight flashed on the windows of the spreading tourist resort buildings between the airstrip and the ocean; that there were flowers everywhere.

Walking from the plane, Karen passed a frangipanni tree with creamy blooms, its branches festooned by a climbing vine bearing masses of golden trumpets. Everything so fragrant . . .

Despite her unhappiness, she felt a lessening of bitterness. Her hand with the flower on its palm was quite steady, fingers curling protectively over the delicate petals.

Pain she still had in plenty. And humiliation . . . But the world was enchanting, the sun warm, the earth fragrant.

For the first time, she believed she could cope with what had happened to her, and whatever she might have to face in the weeks to follow.

She turned to watch the flutterings of a small green butterfly, and the dark man with his grim mouth stood only a few feet away, studying her with his penetrating eyes as if he had read every expression that flitted over her features.

He hadn't spoken on the plane. He had fastened his seat-belt and stared ahead, preoccupied and remote; so Karen didn't smile at him now. She looked away quickly, protecting herself from his curiosity.

She was catching her breath when a gentle voice

asked, 'Are you Miss Fallon? Miss Karen Fallon? I do hope you are.'

She turned swiftly. A boyish-looking man with a young fresh face, a wealth of soft grey hair and gentle pale blue eyes held out his hand.

He repeated, 'I hope you are Miss Fallon,' and to her own surprise Karen found herself smiling back at him, trusting him.

'Yes, I am.'

The clasp of his fingers was just firm enough to be reassuring.

'I'm Victor West. Young Andrew told us you'd be arriving on this plane. It's my aunt, Madeline Hathaway, you'll be looking after. What do you think of the Island?'

'It's quite lovely, what I've seen of it.'

'You haven't had much time to look around yet. We're not far away, at Wapparaburra, but it's too far to carry cases. Miller will drive us. He's collecting your luggage now.'

Karen looked curiously around the tourist resort as they waited for Miller, a widespread complex of residential units, dining-rooms and bars, with occasional small shops and a swimming-pool among coconut palms and tropical gardens.

Miller turned out to be a chunky young man with spiky red hair, short limbs and a healthy, heavy-set body. He had a wide pleasant grin, and he called Karen 'sweetheart' in an inoffensive way that reminded her of the boy next door at home, who had never loved her but had defended her from all who teased when they discovered how vulnerable she was.

Miller drove them in a four-wheel-drive vehicle past the resort and along a glistening white beach, and at the far end of the beach they veered on to a sandy drive into the bushland; and there were banksia trees with golden brushes, scarlet-flowered coral trees, and here and there a poinciana, past flowering now, dangled long leathery pods.

Miller whistled as he drove, and Victor West smiled encouragingly at Karen and said, 'You'll be happy here, I'm sure you will.'

He seemed anxious that she should like what she saw, and Karen wondered what Andrew had told him about her.

As if he read her misgivings Victor added, 'My aunt isn't exactly an invalid. She's recovering after a fairly serious operation, and her doctor wants her to have a long rest away from home. She chose the island, because it's always been her favourite place.'

Karen wondered whether Victor would also be staying with them, but as if he anticipated her question he explained, 'It was awkward for us last week when the previous young lady had to leave. Her mother had an accident and finished up with a broken ankle, so of course Dolly had to go home and care for her. I live and work at Yeppoon on the mainland, and I can slip over here on one of the cruise boats, or the plane from Rockhampton, whenever I have free time; but we're very anxious for my aunt to have someone with her most of the time.' Victor offered Karen a gentle smile. 'That's where you come in.'

'I see. And how long——?'

He seemed vague about the length of her stay. 'It all depends. Three weeks at least, I'd say. I hope that suits you.'

Their redheaded driver pulled up behind a large timbered building surrounded by lawns and trees.

'This is the kiosk and restaurant. I'm getting out here, to pick up some supplies for Aunt Madie; milk and other things.'

Karen waited on the wide verandah of the kiosk

while Victor collected his supplies. She leaned over the railing and watched a flock of rainbow lorikeets, bright green with vivid many-coloured breasts, fluttering around the brushes of a banksia.

She was grateful to Victor for not insisting she go into the kiosk with him; her world had been peopled with strange faces all day, her head ached slightly, her confidence was still shaky.

Victor came out with his purchases, and he and Karen walked together along a winding cement path between low white sandhills covered with bushland, into a valley of trees and exotic gardens, noisy with bird talk.

'Miller has taken your luggage to the cabin. We're along the valley a bit, but not far,' Victor explained.

On the gently sloping hillsides Karen saw a scattering of striped cabins, slanted green roofs among terraced gardens fragrant with frangipanni and hibiscus in an incredible variety of colours, tropical plants in colours and shapes that were almost unreal.

Halfway along the valley Victor led her to a brown and green cabin, calling, 'Here we are, Aunt Madie!' Karen walked ahead of him along a narrow path, across a small patio, through open glass doors into the cabin.

Victor West had talked about his Aunt Madie who was convalescing, Andrew had called her disrespectfully 'the old girl'; but neither man had prepared Karen for the imposing woman who sat writing letters at the table inside the cabin.

Madeline Hathaway was one of the plumpest women Karen had ever seen; there was nothing about her to suggest the wasted invalid she had expected.

Unless, perhaps, the pallor of her beautiful smooth skin, and the faint purple smudges under her eyes, suggested trials endured, a testing of the spirit.

The hair above the high forehead was a sweep of auburn threaded with silver, and her eyes were indomitable. This woman was used to authority.

She wore a long, loose gown in splashy-patterned material, and she moved gracefully, for all her bulk. Her hands were small, with tiny fingers, like dolls' hands.

As Karen came through the doorway Madeline Hathaway said, with friendliness but not too much enthusiasm, 'Let me look at you.'

Karen stood stiffly, bearing the older woman's scrutiny without rancour. If she was to be hired, then she must expect to be examined first ... But she didn't appreciate it. She stood expressionless while Madeline Hathaway studied her.

Then the older woman nodded crisply. 'You'll do,' she announced.

To Karen's surprise she stood up suddenly, very carefully, taking several cautious steps around the table, reaching out a hand to pat Karen's shoulder.

'I expect we'll get along very well together.' The strong mouth curved in a dazzling smile. 'You must excuse my eccentricities, young lady, but I'm something of a recluse at the moment, and we'll be rubbing shoulders together every day. So I want to be sure we can do it amicably, without me exasperating you or——' she touched Karen's hair in a light gesture that was almost affectionate—'without *you* distracting me. And I'm sure we can do it.'

She smiled at her nephew. 'You might pack those things in the refrigerator, Vic.'

She turned to her chair and sat down again, slowly, heavily, as if the effort of walking even those few steps had tired her.

Karen took the supplies from Victor and helped put them away. 'I might as well learn where things go,' she said.

The cabin was divided into three rooms; a bedroom

at either end, with living and cooking space between them, a well furnished kitchen-cum-living-cum-dining area, with a divan, and several chairs around the table, leaving plenty of room for movement.

Miller had already delivered Karen's one suitcase; it stood on the floor of the smaller bedroom and Karen could see it through the open curtains.

Madeline Hathaway asked, 'You'd like to unpack? Victor might get us a cup of tea,' but Victor shook his head.

'Lunch, Aunt Madie—grilled fish with fresh vegetables. You didn't eat breakfast, remember, so you promised to tackle lunch.'

Victor proved a useful man about the house. He showed Karen how to work the stove and griller and the other electrical appliances, and he made helpful suggestions about how to present the food the way his aunt preferred. Yet Madeline ate like a sparrow, protesting that she used so little energy now that she had no need to refuel.

After lunch she wrote more letters, giving them to Victor to post when he left. Then she lay down to rest.

Later that afternoon, Victor left for the mainland on one of the island cruise boats. He held Karen's hand a little longer than was really necessary, promising to come back before the following weekend. He left her a card with his telephone number but assured her he didn't expect any emergencies to arise.

'There's a qualified nurse on Great Keppel, and of course a doctor on the mainland, just a phone call away. But Aunt Madie's past the stage of fearing a relapse or anything like that. She's simply worn out, poor old dear, and there's a spot of high blood pressure to worry about, but she has tablets for that. No wonder she's worn out! Principal of a girls' college for countless years, enough to wear anybody down, if all I hear about modern young misses is half true!' He laughed and touched Karen's arm apologetically. 'I exclude you,' he said. 'I'm certain you're a paragon.' His gentle face creased in a disarming smile. 'And don't let me deter you from telephoning me on the mainland whenever you feel like it. It will be a pleasure and a delight to hear your voice.'

His boyish face flushed. He was very shy, Karen thought. Not glib or confident or persuasive, like Andrew had been, just a pleasant, shy man.

With Victor gone, the valley seemed quieter. Most of the occupants of the other cabins seemed to be away, either on the beaches or exploring the island. Madeline slept, while Karen unpacked as quietly as she could.

Afterwards, sitting in the speckled sunlight on the patio outside the cabin, she stretched her feet and wriggled her toes, watching enchanted as birds flitted about to gather nectar and insects among the trees and flowers.

A black crow sat on a litter-bin staring at her. Just what she didn't need—a bird of ill-omen.

'Go away!' she hissed.

But the crow strutted along the path with brassy confidence, and Karen reached for a pebble from the garden and bowled it towards him.

With an indignant squawk the bird glided to a nearby tree and scolded her. Fearful that Madeline's rest might be disturbed, Karen reached for another pebble, and it was then she glimpsed a hurried movement outside the next cabin. Peering across the tree-screened gardens, she was just in time to glimpse a shadowy figure disappear inside the doorway.

The clustering leaves screened part of the coffee-and-brown cabin from view, but Karen knew she was not mistaken. It was the tall man from the airport, the man with his precious folder of papers, who had whisked himself so smartly back behind his cabin door when he realised she sat there.

She stared at the next cabin resentfully.

'I don't care who you are,' she told it silently. 'If you don't want to be polite and say hello, you needn't. Please feel free to dodge me whenever you fancy. I wouldn't be deprived if I never saw you again!'

But the quiet gully with its secluded cabins and colourful gardens had become suddenly less enchanting. Her sore feelings reacted to the man's withdrawal as if it were yet another rejection, and she scrambled to her feet and went inside, trying not to wonder why the man had hidden himself so quickly when he realised he would have to walk past her on his way to wherever he had intended going.

CHAPTER TWO

AN hour later, Madeline Hathaway awoke, after what she claimed to be the most refreshing sleep she had had for many days. She let Karen dress her again in the long bright gown, and brush her hair, then take her for a short walk along the narrow path that snaked its way between cabins.

They didn't walk far, but it was enough to bring faint colour to her pale cheeks, and afterwards they sat outside together, and people coming back from the beaches smiled and waved to Madeline as they passed.

Karen prepared their evening meal from what she found in the cabin. There were steaks in the fridge, plenty of fresh vegetables, fruit salad, and ice cream in the freezer. Victor had left plenty of everything.

After the meal Madeline said, 'You're a clever little cook, Karen.'

'I didn't make the fruit salad. I found it in the fridge.'

'Doesn't matter. Those steaks were delicious. I didn't feel at all hungry until I tasted them.'

Madeline relaxed in her chair, drinking coffee, smiling at Karen with friendly curiosity.

'Do you want to tell me about yourself?'

Karen tensed. She had known she would eventually have to explain how she came to be here, but suddenly her mind went blank. She couldn't talk about it now. It would have to wait until the wound healed.

She replied evasively, 'There's nothing to tell, really. Just—nothing.'

'All right.' Madeline surveyed her discomfiture with friendly compassionate eyes. 'I wasn't trying to pry, my dear.'

'I know.' Impulsively Karen leaned towards her, curling her fingers around the small hand. 'I've only just arrived here from England, a couple of days ago.'

'So recently?'

'Yes. I was—planning to meet up with—with a friend. only my friend——' Karen swallowed uneasily, 'my friend wasn't available. And I heard about this job from—from someone—and that's it. If you don't want me, I can look for somewhere else—another place——'

Her voice trailed off miserably. Madeline protested warmly, 'Of course I want you. I told you, I believe we'll get along very well together. I understand from Victor that you came with a most enthusiastic reference.' Her voice was carefully casual as she added, 'From a family Victor knows well.'

Karen drew in a long, deep, steadying breath. Now she would have to say his name.

'Andrew Pinnar. I met him in England.' She couldn't believe how unemotional her own voice sounded, how cool, how uninvolved.

'Yes,' Madeline nodded cheerfully. 'So that settles it, doesn't it? And will you call me Madeline, please. To my family I've always been Madie; but it brings back recollections of my girls at college. So I prefer the full name, if you don't mind.'

'Madeline—it's a pretty name, I like it.'

Madeline lifted her arms, with their bright and billowing sleeves, linking her fingers behind her elegant head. She pursed her lips, her face alight with amusement.

'Can you imagine what they called me, the girls in college, with a name like mine?'

Karen wrinkled her forehead. 'Madeline Hathaway,' she murmured slowly. 'No, I can't. It doesn't suggest anything particularly.'

'Then you aren't nearly as devilishly inventive as my ingenious young ladies.' Madeline chuckled. 'They called me the Mad Hatter. That's what they christened me, from the first day I took my place behind the principal's desk in that decorous school for young ladies. The Mad Hatter. I wasn't supposed to know, and of course I always pretended I didn't hear it. But I'm afraid it stuck.' Her face lit up with mirth. 'Sometimes, even now, when I'm out shopping I hear somebody whisper, 'Hey, isn't that the Mad Hatter?' Of course, I always do my best to look invisible when I hear it, but that's not too easy when you're my size, and people often turn and stare.'

'We had names for most of our teachers,' Karen remembered. 'Of course, we always thought they were secret, but I suppose they never are.'

However low her spirits, it was impossible not to respond to Madeline's friendly curiosity.

As she cleared away Karen silently thanked her mother for a good basic training in housework and cooking. There didn't seeem very much to do here, but she wanted to do it well.

Looking out through the cabin windows she saw splashes of crimson sky between trees. So it was sunset. The most disastrous day of her life was ending.

Madeline came out of her bedroom with an armful of books. 'Need any reading material, Karen, or did you come prepared?'

Karen confessed that she hadn't thought about reading matter.

'Then help yourself. There's a couple of Agatha Christies, if you like a good mystery. Or a travel book. Plus a collection of Australian short stories. Take whichever one interests you.'

Madeline spread the books on the table.

'I'm a mystery freak myself. I don't think you can beat a good murder for relaxation. But you're not ready to settle down and read yet, are you? Why don't you get a breath of fresh air? Take a walk along the beach.'

'Wouldn't you like me to stay with you? I'm not being much help.'

Madeline's smile flashed.

'You're doing all that's needed, my dear, just by being here. My fussy family won't let me stay alone until I get the results of my next medical examination. So I'm grateful to you for coming, otherwise I'd have been yanked back into the busy world, which is just what I don't want at present. Rest is all I need—rest, and no problems. Nothing to tax my collapsed resources.'

Karen looked disbelievingly at the calm face.

'Have they really collapsed?'

'Slightly rocked, shall we say.' Madeline's shoulders shrugged. 'Yes, they did get jolted a bit. There I was sailing through life, simply bursting with good health, sixty years young,' she remembered. 'Then one day, along comes a twinge, then some more twinges, finally an operation that may or may not prove successful.

You don't believe it, you know, when they tell you that. Suddenly, out of the blue, no matter how energetic you feel, you have to face the fact that there's a chance you may not have many tomorrows left.'

Again she shrugged, this time with a smile.

'As it happens, my operation looks like being one hundred per cent successful. I'll know for sure after the next medical check-up, they tell me. But my faith in the future received an almighty jolt. Sometimes I wonder if I'll ever really feel secure again. Not so often now, but sometimes I sit and ponder about how close I've been to seeing it all slip away. All the glorious things I planned to do in my retirement——' She laughed wryly at Karen. 'A fine conversation this is! Don't let me depress you. I'm fast becoming invigorated. Now and again my spirits need lifting, that's all. Don't worry, I'll tell you when it happens. I'll say: Talk to me, Karen. Or read to me. Just some little thing to hold back the gloom. You'll know when I need your company. I'll ask——'

Karen reached for one of the Agatha Christie mysteries. 'I think I should stay with you now.'

'Indeed you shouldn't. I'm not that melancholy, not this evening. In fact, I feel remarkably healthy. Go on out, and enjoy your walk. If you walk down past the kiosk, you can choose between two beaches, Fishermen's Beach with the resort alongside it, and Putney Beach on the other side of the spit.'

Karen walked out of the valley, across the dunes, to where she found the sunset splashing scarlet in the sky, rose-red in the reflecting sea.

She glanced along the beach at the coloured lights of the resort glittering in the early twilight, but decided against it, turning instead to the long curve of pearly beach that stretched beside Wapparaburra.

As she walked, the red plumes of sunset waved

behind mountains on the mainland; and slowly twilight
deepened to dusk, the colours faded from the sky, and
still she walked, occasionally passing clumps of trees
with slender, drooping foliage.

A light wind skittered off the ocean and wailed in
the graceful trees, and Karen found the sound suitably
mournful. It fitted in with her mood as she walked
along the quiet beach.

Although she had smothered her heartache in the
day's activities it was still there, stirring her emotions,
waiting to show itself whenever she allowed it. She was
still vulnerable. More so now, perhaps, because she had
time on this peaceful walk to face the bitter disappointment, the collapse of all the bright dreaming Andrew
had aroused in her so easily while he was in England.

Although the evening was not cold, she shivered.
She hadn't needed Andrew's reactions to tell her she
had made a fool of herself, and but for Madeline
Hathaway she would right now be preparing to get on
a plane and fly back home, trying to explain to friends
and family just how foolish she had been, how very
naïve, and how trusting.

Andrew hadn't hesitated to reject her. 'That ought
to say something about my charms,' she told herself
with bitter humour. 'Instantaneous rejection after
travelling halfway around the world!'

Wrapped in her reflections, she almost failed to
notice the dark smudge of a small boat on the water's
edge at the far end of the beach as she approached.
She had veered closer to the bushland, away from the
shoreline, and the small craft lay not more than a few
yards ahead of her when she discovered it. In the stern,
Karen saw the gleam of curly blonde hair, the outline
of a blurred, slender figure.

As she paused to try and see it more closely in the
dimness, Karen heard the snapping of dry twigs in

bushland behind her. A man moved among the confusing shadows of a grove of the same drooping trees she had heard wailing in the wind. He carried a pair of oars, and because he wore dark clothing his figure blended with the dusk and the tree-shadows, but his shape was unmistakable. The lean shoulders, slender hips, long, long legs, now in denim jeans, the rumpled brown hair flopping darkly over the high forehead, curling on the nape of the neck.

It was the man from the airport, the stranger from the next cabin.

Karen stared at him dumbly as he walked towards her. Everything was black and grey and pearly-white; the figure of the man, too, stayed draped in shadow as he halted not far away from her, still in the shelter of the trees.

He glowered at her from under dark, winged eyebrows, out of those black eyes; and she glared resentfully back at him. How dared he come loping out of the darkness to interrupt her grief?

'You again!' He didn't sound exactly delighted to find her here. And when she said nothing, he made a swift hissing sound through lips and teeth, as though it worried him that she should be about.

'If anybody asks,' he announced finally, 'you haven't seen me here. Think you can remember that?'

He sounded brisk and peremptory, like a sergeant-major giving orders to his troops. Karen came out of her reverie and faced him with defiance.

'I can see you,' she contradicted. 'I see you very clearly. And if anybody asks me, I shall say so.'

He considered her thoughtfully, assessing her expression as well as he could through the dusk between them. Then he carefully put down the oars he carried, and this time his voice was harsh.

'I repeat, you have not seen me.'

Somewhere deep under pain and humiliation, anger exploded in Karen. She lifted her face to his, bracing herself, almost as if she expected him to strike her.

'Don't tell me what to do!' she flared. 'I know what I can see. And if anybody asks me, I've seen you, skulking about in the bushes——'

The man took a sudden step towards her, until he was so close she heard his breathing. He reached out an arm and jerked her roughly towards him. The denim jacket he wore hung open, and she found herself thrust hard against a muscled body that felt strangely rigid against her own. The light cotton dress she wore was no barrier against the contact.

She became aware of a shock impact, as if somebody had snapped her to attention by sudden loud noise. She was imprisoned in long hard arms, jolted out of self-pity into the sharp realisation that she was here on the beach with a man, alone except for the distant person in the boat, who seemed to be unaware of what was going on.

The man held her hard against him until she thought she must suffocate.

'Maybe I can persuade you.' His voice was silky. 'Is that what I have to do? I suppose it must be, since a polite request won't work.'

'A polite request!' Karen twisted in a frantic effort at escape, but the man moved an implacable hand, fingers outspread and curved to shape the back of her neck, holding her prisoner. Above her the dark face gleamed in a brief smile of malicious pleasure.

'This could be quite enjoyable,' he drawled, as his mouth came down hard on her muffled protests.

There was no one on the beach to help her. To the person in the dinghy, they must be invisible among the shadowy trees.

Karen made another effort to pull away, but the arms

around her tightened, the mouth pressed against her own lips preventing outcry. The man had suggested the experience might be enjoyable, but this was punishment kissing, his mouth hard, impatient, threatening bruises unless she yielded. Karen pressed her lips tightly together and her tormentor lifted his head, teeth flashing white as he jibed at her attempts to repel him.

'Keep fighting me,' his voice jeered. 'Who knows what it might lead to, Golden Hair?' His laughter derisive. 'It's up to you how long it takes to get your co-operation. I've got all the time in the world.'

This time his mouth came down on hers slowly, and because she was apprehensive, Karen's lips parted, so that the act became more like a kissing, less of a threat, yet not like any other kissing she had ever known.

The contact sparked a quivering reaction that set her whole body suddenly alert, as if somebody had suddenly and sharply drawn all her attention together, so that she became totally aware of just this one happening—the body contact between herself and the stranger.

She felt the world spin and falter, before her awareness narrowed down so that there was nothing in the universe, no sky, no trees, no past, no future; only the powerful body pressing against hers, the kissing so vibrant it set every nerve in her body trembling and aware.

When he let her go, she summoned just enough control to screen her reactions from his shrewd and searching scrutiny. He hesitated, one hand still touching her shoulder, fingers trailing on the soft skin of her neck.

Then he spoke slowly. 'Something for us both to remember.' His voice was low, indistinct in the gathering dark, his touch so light, so fragile, that Karen

could have pulled away, except that her will refused to
make the effort.

She didn't want to break the contact. She realised
with startled wonder that this was the most explosive
thing that had ever happened to her, the most inexplicable. Her whole body, every nerve and every cell,
was responding to the touch of a total stranger.

She put out a shaking hand, fingers clutching the
denim jacket as though she might have fallen. As if it
were a signal he drew in a deep long breath and
deliberately detached himself, slowly, carefully,
steadying her. Or was he steadying himself?

He turned his head towards the dinghy in the water,
at the blonde head of its only occupant shining palely
in the first starlight.

'Remember,' he reminded Karen slowly, 'you
haven't seen me, or the boat. I haven't been here.'

'No,' Karen said bitterly. 'I hate you. I haven't seen
you.'

Still he remained unsatisfied. He moved a few paces
away, watching her thoughtfully, breathing fast as if
he too may have been shaken by the encounter.

But of course he wasn't. He had needed to make a
point, and he had made it. Using coercion, when force
failed . . . manipulating, to get his own way . . .

'You aren't going to tell anybody you saw me here.
Are you?'

'All right.' Karen flung the words at him sharply. 'I
haven't seen you. I give you my word, if that will
satisfy you. Do you want me to cross my heart, or
something?'

'No, your word will do.'

He bent to pick up the oars. Then he stepped farther
away, brushing the hair back from his forehead with
his free hand, watching her carefully.

Karen was horrified to find herself shrieking at him.

'Go away!' she cried. 'You're loathsome! Odious—objectionable——'

He gave her a look of derision.

'Sorry I can't return the compliment,' he drawled, 'but I don't find you repulsive at all. That was quite an experience, Miss Golden Hair.'

He strode across the white sand to the small boat. Karen heard the rattle of oars as he stowed them away before pushing the boat on to the water. She listened for the murmur of voices, but there was no sound until the motor crackled into life and the small craft shot away.

Spellbound, she gazed after it, watching it make a wide curve as it swept out to sea; and still she stood there, powerless to move, until it disappeared behind rocks at the far end of the beach, and was swallowed up in darkness. Wherever he was going, the man seemed determined to get there quickly.

The boat's disappearance released her from her trance. She remembered Madeline Hathaway, and realised she had been away longer than she intended. She made a tremendous effort to discipline the treacherous beating of her heart, the shaking of her fingers. She moistened her lips with her tongue, her lips that were still warm from the kissing of a man she did not know.

She didn't even know his name, but she was sure of one thing: that he was a dangerous man, a man from far outside the experience of her own limited world.

You could find yourself afraid of this man, she decided. Terribly, desperately afraid.

She turned and walked back towards Wapparaburra, following the pattern of her own footsteps on the sand, until she reached the access track to the valley.

Then she wended her way over the dunes, past the tents of campers in one small gully, up again to the

sloping hillsides with their terraced gardens and the
cabin lights glimmering among the trees.

Lights glowed golden along the paths, and from
inside the green and brown cabin where Madeline
waited for her, Karen saw the windows glow with
warmth and welcome, beaming out a message of sanc-
tuary. She found herself hurrying towards it as if it
were the most important signal she would ever receive.

CHAPTER THREE

KAREN'S sleep that night was psychedelic. No black
and white dreams, these, but disruptive flashes of
colour, a jarring display of scenes that jerked her awake
time after time.

Although the Wapparaburra valley was sheltered
from ocean winds, there were countless times when
Karen found herself wakened suddenly, as if she had
been aroused by some strange sound, only to discover
it was the product of her imagination. There were no
noises outside. The valley lay quiet all around her.

Several times she woke, groping for reality as she
tried to remember where she was, and why. Sometimes
her mind fumbled dizzily for the feel of the plane, not
finding it. At other times she lay staring at the pale
shape of her window, while her memory stumbled
through the events of yesterday, putting her life together only to have it fall apart when reality intruded.

This must be jet-lag. She remembered hearing how
people sometimes become confused after long plane
journeys; she had heard about the loss of time sense,
the lack of orientation.

So she knew what was wrong with her, didn't she?

Not fear, not insecurity, but jet-lag. Sometimes she longed for a torch so that she could press the button and summon the friendly cabin walls around her. She dared not creep out of bed to turn on the light; to disturb Madeline would be disastrous.

But dawn brought stability. It even brought sweetness. A brown bird sat in a paperbark tree and from his tiny throat came a rise and fall of sound like flute music. Other birds added their distinctive calls. The rising sun deepened from pearl to gold, while Karen watched the strange new world take shape around her.

She checked her wristwatch, making sure it was a reasonable time for breakfast before she got out of bed to shower and dress.

It took a lot of persuasion to coax Madeline to eat breakfast. All she wanted was a cup of coffee, but Karen recalled Victor's instructions and finally persuaded her to accept orange juice, with cereal and milk and a slice of toast, before she produced the coffee.

'You're bossy.' Madeline's smile took the sting out of her protest. 'Giving orders is my prerogative—or it should be.'

She displayed her ample figure, swathed in another colourful gown. 'I can't be ill. I'm not wasting away.'

Karen laughed. 'You could waste away,' she threatened, 'if you limit yourself to cups of coffee.'

Madeline smoothed the flowing folds of her bright robe. 'I wear the most unsuitable gear for an old lady. I thought I'd point it out in case you hadn't noticed.' Her eyes twinkled. 'After a lifetime of tailored suits and blouses I felt entitled to splash in my retirement. There isn't a gown in my wardrobe that doesn't float, swing or flounce. I wonder if I've been repressed, all those years of standing on my dignity.'

Karen put away the last dish, wiped down the table. 'You'd be foolish if you wore anything more severe.

Those bright floaty gowns suit you.'

'They camouflage my size, you mean.' Madeline's smile was a chuckle. 'Meanwhile, my child, why don't you go for a walk and buy yourself a gorgeous bikini? You could have a swim in that lovely blue sea.'

'No, thanks.' Karen set a bowl of fruit in the centre of the table. 'I'll make the beds, then I thought you could use my services one way or another.'

'I shan't need you in constant attendance, my dear. And you can't make beds this morning. Jenna calls to change the linen today. You can do them tomorrow. I'll take a stroll to the kiosk to get some postcards, then come back to my embroidery. That's my schedule for the next few weeks, I'm afraid, reading, writing and sewing.'

'Can I get the postcards for you?'

'No, thanks. That little jaunt to the shop each morning sets me up for the day. Then I sit outside and do some needlework while you go off on your own for a couple of hours.' She smiled cheerfully. 'Take yourself off for another walk if you feel like it. This is a large island, with plenty of places to explore.'

While Madeline was away Karen washed her hair, changed into a pink and white sundress that might let the pale skin of her arms and shoulders tan a little, then set up folding table and chairs outside on the patio.

Madeline was still absent when a tall, dark-tanned girl with a swinging ponytail of black hair wheeled her cleaning trolley to a halt outside the cabin.

'Hi, I'm Jenna, otherwise known as Sadie the cleaning lady. I call every few days with clean linen, fresh tea-towels and suchlike. You'll be seeing lots of me.'

Cheerfully Jenna carried her bundle into the cabin, glancing curiously at Karen, who followed her in.

'You're the new lass looking after Miss Hathaway?'

'That's right. Karen Fallon.'

They smiled at each other.

'She's a doll, isn't she, your Miss Hathaway?' Jenna stripped beds expertly while she talked. 'You'll love it here—we all do. How long are you staying?'

'I don't know,' Karen confessed. 'I—I only got the job unexpectedly—and—I think it's to be just as long as Miss Hathaway needs me. I've only been in this country a few days.'

'Well, let's hope it's a while.' Jenna moved swiftly from one room to the other. 'Plenty to see and do, lots of people to meet. You won't be bothered with noise, you've got quiet neighbours, especially the mystery man. *He* won't keep you awake nights. I don't know why he bothers to rent his cabin. He hardly ever uses it.'

'You mean the tall man next door?'

'That's him. Dain Lammont, or whatever he's calling himself this time.'

Karen straightened herself curiously. 'You mean he uses other names? Why does he do that?'

Jenna glanced quickly at Karen as she stripped down the second bed. Her expression was suddenly reserved, as if she might have regretted her impulsive confidence.

'I don't know.' It seemed to Karen she was being deliberately vague. 'Nothing to bother about, I suppose. He never worries anyone. Just picks up his mail, has an occasional meal, then disappears.'

She tossed the used linen on to her trolley. 'How about coming to a party tonight?' she added quickly, 'unless you're doing anything else.' Karen shook her head, and Jenna laughed.

'Haven't you been discovered yet?' She was looking appreciatively at Karen's slender figure in the pink and white dress, at the sheen of long yellow hair, the delicate heart-shaped face. 'You will be. Just wait till the boys get a load of your pretty face!'

Karen flushed. 'I don't think I should leave Miss Hathaway——'

'She probably wouldn't miss you for an hour or so, if you'd like to drop in. I'll talk to her about it, if you like.'

Jenna kept a caring watch over all the occupants of the cabins. When they left at the end of their holidays she always said warmly, 'Come again next year,' and they usually did.

She was thinking that Karen looked as if she could do with a little loving care herself, and wondered why she had accepted work so quickly, instead of taking time off for a holiday after her arrival in a strange country.

She said, 'You won't forget the party?'

A party, or any other kind of festivity, was something Karen didn't desire any part of at present, but she didn't want to sound ungrateful.

She asked politely, 'Where is it?' and Jenna explained, 'In the gardens behind the kiosk. There's a wooden rotunda among the trees; that's our bar. And we have a barbecue. So we all sit around and talk our heads off, and maybe Miller will play his guitar. It's quite informal.'

'Won't anybody mind me coming? I mean, I'm a stranger.'

Jenna smiled. 'It's my party,' she explained. 'My twenty-third birthday. I celebrated the last one in South America, and the one before that in the Seychelle Islands. I was born here on Great Keppel, but sometimes I get the wanders and take off for a while, though I always come back.' She patted the cabin door affectionately. 'Always. So see if you can call in, even if it's only for a few minutes tonight, and drink a toast to me and my birthday.'

Madeline, meeting Jenna as she wheeled her trolley on to the pathway, decided Karen should go to the party.

'Of course you must. Agatha Christie and I will both keep. I'll read her first, and promise not to tell you if the butler did it.'

Karen found herself being gently pressed against her will in a direction she decidedly didn't want to go.

She said helplessly, 'Perhaps for a few minutes,' because they were kind.

She knew exactly how she would feel, watching couples at a party, seeing the intimate smiles, the tenderness between people, all the things she had expected to share with Andrew. The touch of love and warmth and caring.

She would much rather stay with Madeline. Besides, that was her job.

Jenna went on her way to the quiet cabin next door. It looked deserted. Wherever the tall man and his blonde companion had gone last night, it seemed they had not returned.

A flock of lorikeets, flashes of emerald green, had settled in a tree in the dividing garden. They were apparently quite accustomed to finding this cabin deserted. When Jenna walked down the path to the doorway they flew off reluctantly, eyeing her from other trees in the bushland as if she were the intruder, not they.

Karen wondered why she was letting the empty cabin intrigue her. She wasn't a curious person. The lean man with his forbidding expression, his reticence and his arrogance, meant nothing to her except for a couple of unpleasant experiences she would prefer to forget.

But Jenna had labelled him a mystery man, who used

not one name, but several. And he had been so very off-putting when Karen reached out to pick up the papers she had caused him to scatter around the airport. As if he didn't want her to see them.

Jenna produced a pass-key and let herself into the cabin, and Karen went inside to help Madeline carry out her embroidery materials.

She exclaimed, 'Wow—petit-point! I'm impressed. My mother can do that kind of needlework, but I've never had enough time or patience.'

And Madeline answered drily, 'I have all the time in the world, and I'm learning to be patient. Although I must admit I'm getting slightly bored with roses and trees and cottages.' 'I've produced cushion covers for all my friends, and decked my family's dining chairs with fancy seats. I'll have to branch out into something different very soon.'

She spread out her work on the table for Karen to look at. Not all petit-point; she had worked in a variety of stitches, and there were two wall hangings that must have taken hours of patient work.

Karen felt a stab of pity. How confined Madeline must have felt, pouring all the energy she had used in her work among college students and staff into this solitary occupation, sitting still, when she had been used to activity.

She stroked the outline of a flower arrangement with appreciative fingers.

'It's very beautiful. Some day you'll be proud of all that work.'

With Madeline settled on the patio, Karen found herself despatched to the kiosk to telephone Victor for some embroidery cottons and wool Madeline had decided she must have as soon as possible.

Karen wasn't sure she wanted to ring Victor quite so soon. He was a nice, decent, friendly person; but she wasn't in the market for too much friendliness just at the moment.

She wanted to avoid anything but the most casual contact with the human race, while she sorted out her twisted emotions, but she couldn't refuse to call Madeline's nephew.

Victor was delighted to hear Karen's voice, once he established that there was no emergency. Too delighted, Karen feared. Her over-sensitive feelings picked up the impression that he thought her call was made because she wanted to talk with him.

She hung up the telephone uneasily, and the girl behind the counter called, 'Hello, I'm Gracie. You're Miss Hathaway's new companion, I guess. Welcome to the island. Are you coming to Jenna's birthday celebrations tonight?'

Karen said yes, she might call in for a few minutes. Here she was, doing her best to shrink away from people, and everyone she met offered friendly advances, so that she had this awful feeling that to withhold herself was hostile and unworthy, yet what else could she do while she wept inwardly?

She walked back through the speckled sunlight of the gardens, stepping on tree shadows, remnants of jet-lag confusion taunting her, so that she wanted to run anywhere but towards the cabin and the commitment she had made to stay in Australia instead of going home.

But Madeline sat outside the brown and green cabin, busy with embroidery, and her greeting brought her sharply down to earth.

'He's here!' Madeline nodded haughtily towards the nearby cabin. 'That Lammont person. Stalked right past with nothing but a twitchy duck of his head. Horrid, unfriendly man!'

Madeline didn't like Dain Lammont. She preferred

the friendly young couple in the cabin across the next garden behind them, who might have been honeymooners. Or the group of teenagers in the next cabin but one, who played pop music and never failed to stop and talk to her when they passed.

There were four young men in one of the other cabins; they spent the daylight hours fishing from their yacht, and sometimes they brought home fish which they shared with everybody. In the evenings they went to the kiosk to listen to Miller play his guitar, or to the resort, and sometimes, Madeline said, they brought home pretty girls.

On her better days Madeline took a lively interest in the people around her. This morning she entertained Karen with as much of their histories as she had been able to glean.

But whenever she spoke of Dain Lammont her voice chilled. Never once had he paused to talk with her about the needlework she did, or to discuss what a delightful winter it could be if you were able to spend it basking on an island in Queensland, away from the southern cities where the wind was bleak and cold rain fell down in buckets.

Many of the people in the cabins and at the nearby resort, Madeline explained, were southerners who had fled harsh winters.

But Dain Lammont told nobody where he came from nor why he was here; nor was he likely to explain why he bothered to rent a cabin at all when his visits were so fleeting.

'A Heathcliff of a man,' Madeline complained crossly, looking over at the other cabin with its window drapes pulled across the glass, although the man was in there. She looked at Karen, her glance quizzical. 'You recall your Emily Brontë, I presume?' Karen said yes, she had studied *Wuthering Heights* at school.

She comprehended instantly why Madeline had labelled Dain Lammont 'a Heathcliff of a man'. The taciturn expression, the repelling dark face with its hooded eyes, his determined lack of friendliness.

'That's a very bitter man,' Madeline elaborated. 'A cruel man, too, I shouldn't be surprised.'

Karen said, 'Never mind, he won't bother us.' She gave Madeline a determined smile. 'I don't care if he's Bluebeard or the Hound of the Baskervilles. You can't let him spoil your enjoyment.'

And suddenly she knew it was true. Not Dain Lammont, nor Andrew, nor her own heartbreak, should be allowed to bring sorrow into this pleasant valley. She smiled brightly at Madeline and said, 'I'll put the kettle on,' and later while she sat helping Madeline sort embroidery threads she found that somewhere deep in her mind a decision had been made.

If it were possible, she would take her first step back into the mainstream of life by slipping away for half an hour tonight to Jenna's party.

However, there was to be no 'slipping away.' Rather, Karen was to set out in a fanfare of fussing. Because just before the evening meal there came the crunch of footsteps outside, and Victor appeared, smiling gently, pleased with himself, holding out the materials Madeline had asked for.

'No trouble,' he insisted, when Madeline protested. 'A mate of mine came over in his yacht, he's brought some material for his house. So I thumbed a ride, or a sail if you prefer, and I'm staying with Les overnight and sailing back in the morning.'

Madeline didn't hide her satisfaction.

'You can take Karen to Jenna's birthday party. I hope you've brought something pretty to wear, my child.'

Victor smiled at Karen.

'It won't be that kind of party, Aunt Madie. I know Jenna and her celebrations. It'll be jeans and T-shirts, and a lovely relaxed evening sitting around the rotunda with a drink in one hand and a roast chicken leg in the other.'

'You'd better not eat too much dinner, then.' Madeline's eyes twinkled. 'Are you eating with us?'

'No. Sorry, Aunt Madie, I promised to have dinner with Les. I'll be back afterwards to collect Karen and take her to the party.'

Karen mused uneasily that she would have preferred to call in on Jenna's celebrations alone. Victor was very kind, but intuition warned her that Madeline might be matchmaking. She talked all through the evening meal about her nephew, how thoughtful he was beneath his shyness, and how clever.

'A scholar,' she explained, sighing a little, because Victor's scholarly pursuits had not brought him into much contact with girls; and Victor would some day make somebody a splendid husband.

'Victor always was a thinker,' Madeline went on. 'Always something of a dreamer. And dreamers are apt to be overlooked alongside the more obvious attractions of today's extroverted males.'

After dinner, Madeline announced that she would need no further attention, so Karen dressed in pink denim jeans and a rose-coloured T-shirt with long sleeves, and soon found herself being escorted through the gardens by Victor, then sitting at ease with a crowd of young people who milled around, talking and laughing under the garden lights.

People came to chat with Victor, and stayed to talk to Karen. Later, when Karen made an attempt to leave and visit Madeline, Victor pressed her down onto the seat, and went himself to the cabin.

'Talk to Miller,' he ordered gently, and Miller said. 'That's right, darling, talk to Miller. He's harmless, not like some we know.'

He directed an over-acted mock leer at the nearest young male who was edging towards Karen; and Karen found that talking to Miller was easy, because all she had to do was listen.

Miller was diverting, entertaining, and when Victor came back he found Karen more animated. For the first time, she had actually laughed.

'Aunt Madie's reading in bed,' he reported. 'She said to enjoy yourself. I've given her a mug of cocoa and she wants nothing more until morning.'

Victor had done more than that. He confided that he had talked to his aunt about Karen's free time, and now he asked Miller, 'How about teaching Karen to handle your small boat? My aunt thinks it would be an excellent idea,' and to Karen, 'You can swim, I hope?'

Karen said yes, she could swim, and before she knew what was happening he and Miller were making arrangements for her to have lessons in handling the boat if the sea was still calm next morning. When she protested he said, 'My aunt doesn't want you underfoot all the time. You're supposed to have some leisure, and she likes some time to herself. So when she prefers to be alone you can hire the boat and have a look at some of the other islands. Or you can cruise from one beach to another. Sometimes it's quicker than walking.'

Later, Miller went away and came back with an enormous birthday cake, and Karen saw with startled wonder that it was almost midnight, and the evening she had dreaded had gone by pleasantly.

Jenna made her wait for a slice of birthday cake, and while she cut it Miller played his guitar, and Victor took her to the wooden rotunda to show her the carvings that decorated almost all of it.

'All the work of one man, Francis Taupongi. He came from one of the Solomon Islands.'

And Jenna interrupted, 'You should have been here a few weeks ago, then you'd have met him. he didn't want to leave,' she confided to Victor. 'Miller swears he had tears in his eyes when he left. He'll be back of course. I told you, we all come back.'

Francis Taupongi, they told Karen, had been a laughing, dark-skinned man with a mop of black curly hair and a flashing smile; and the hands of Francis Taupongi had been truly gifted. Skilfully and patiently he had created his polished carvings—an owl with haunted yellow eyes; an eagle grasping a snake in curved talons; a sea-snake curled around the centre-pole from thatched roof to the ground. An Island chief stared out with hauteur at the milling throng around him, and a crocodile basked with deceptive languor alongside a barramundi with gleaming scales.

'What fascinating things to leave behind you.' Karen touched the carved feathers of the owl appreciatively, and Victor laughed and said, 'You haven't left us yet. Who knows what you may leave behind you? Or take with you.'

Then he looked at her quickly and blushed, and Karen said quickly, 'Victor, I really must go back to your aunt.'

He held her arm lightly all the way back to the cabin, a courteous hand cupping her elbow as if she were something precious and fragile, and Karen realised thankfully that she could not invite him inside, because Madeline would be asleep.

He hesitated, as if he might have said more than just goodnight, then he said, 'I'll see you again very soon, Karen. I shall look forward to it.'

Karen watched him walk away, half uneasy, half

grateful because he had given her the first respite from tormenting emotions, and he was gentle and courteous and kind, and she didn't want to hurt him in any way.

Before she settled down for the night, she crept outside to hang out her towel on the railing of the patio.

She glanced along the pathway, just in time to glimpse two figures crossing from the bushland towards one of the access tracks to the beach.

They looked far away in the darkness as she stared down the narrow path, trees enclosing it like a gold-lighted tunnel; but she recognised the man.

It was Dain Lammont. He had the same small blonde companion, and he did not look up to see Karen standing among the shadowy gardens.

She crept inside to bed and lay there, wondering why she felt so disturbed because Dain Lammont was not lying peacefully in his cabin, but moving about in the darkness, bound for some secret place that had nothing to do with this enchanted valley. And, she honestly admitted, nothing to do with her either.

Yet still she lay there, clutching at sleep but having it evade her, because two people she did not know had moved among the shadows of the bushland, and she could not imagine where they were going, or why.

CHAPTER FOUR

MILLER'S boat, Karen discovered next day, was a four-metre aluminium dinghy with outboard motor, a small craft by island standards but ideal for skipping from one island to another, or from beach to beach around the winding shores and headlands of Great Keppel Island.

Miller gave Karen lessons on gentle seas during the next few days, mostly in the afternoons while Madeline rested. Karen hesitated about leaving the cabin, it seemed to her like desertion, but Madeline shooed her away.

'Off you go, young lady,' she urged. 'I don't require you pussyfooting around while I'm sleeping. I'll expect you back in a couple of hours. Go and learn to take care of yourself in the boat, and I hope you enjoy it, so long as you don't invite me out in that cockleshell!'

Karen offered to reimburse Miller for boat hire and fuel, but he shrugged and said, 'All taken care of. Victor says, put it on his account.'

Karen, wanting to be independent, made a silent resolution to see Victor about payment, because it made her uneasy to owe him anything more than the pay he had already arranged to give her.

But the ocean was calm and bright and Karen forgot her qualms. She learned quickly, adapting easily to the behaviour of the boat under the influence of wind and water, and soon Miller pronounced her a 'natural.'

Several afternoons later, he let her take over while they travelled around the island, making sure she understood the special caution required rounding each headland, where currents and conditions changed from one beach to another.

There were all kinds of craft on the waters, from sleek yachts and fishermen's trawlers to the one-man leisure 'toys' of holidaymakers. Outside the palm-fringed holiday resort, windsurfers darted over the ocean like bright-winged butterflies. From Miller's boatshed at Wapparaburra, jet-ski riders cut swift white curves on blue water.

Sun on her face, wind blowing her hair, Karen steered Miller's boat, watching with envy the antics of windsurfers and jet-ski riders.

'You'll learn to handle both if you stay here long,' Miller promised, but she shook her head doubtfully.

'Those windsurfers aren't as easy as they look. I watched a girl learning yesterday and she spent half her time capsized in the water.'

'There's a knack. You'll master it in an hour, I give you my word.'

'I have a lot to learn,' Karen admitted wistfully, and Miller grinned.

'More than you think,' he agreed. 'But you're already an ace with the boat, so you shouldn't have trouble with anything else. Why don't you stay on here a while after you finish your job with Miss Hathaway?'

Karen had not considered what she would do, or where she might go, when Madeline Hathaway no longer needed her. She had shut her mind right now to the future and its decisions, pretending they were far away.

She had another hour in the boat before Madeline expected her, and she would enjoy every minute.

There were seventeen miles of white beaches around Great Keppel Island, Miller told her, as he pointed out a sea eagle's nest on a headland, and later showed her the steep grassy slopes where the island's wild goats grazed, safe from intrusion.

'And there are thirty-four islands in Keppel Bay,' he added. 'All named and counted, but not by me.'

They passed several beaches with groves of the slender drooping trees that had sighed in the wind—casuarinas, Miller told her. Then he took over the boat and headed out to sea. He travelled fast and Karen found herself clinging to the sides of the boat as it skimmed across the water, aluminium bows thumping as it bounced across waves.

'I promised Jenna some oysters,' Miller shouted.

'And I know the place to get them, on one of the islands.'

'I'll help you.'

He glanced quickly at Karen's feet, bare except for gold-strapped thongs.

'Not this time. It's too rugged for that sort of foot-wear. Next time wear sandshoes or something like that and I'll let you play helper.'

He waved at island shapes as they sped past. 'If you see any place you'd like to explore let me know. I'll drop you off and pick you up on my way back. Not nervous, are you, being left on your own?'

Karen said no, she wasn't nervous. She was about to tell Miller to choose any island he fancied, when they approached the odd silhouette of a tiny scrap of land. In the blue distance it had seemed to sit on the sea like a toadstool, overhanging clifftops jutting out above eroded rocks; but as they drew nearer she saw the shape was an illusion. The black rocks only seemed to recede, as their darkness clashed with the light-coloured land above them.

A ray of the sun flashed on something in the sky, a swift sudden glint that quickly vanished, but it captured Karen's attention and she frowned into the strong sunlight.

'Blunteree,' Miller followed her glance. 'Unoccupied, and pretty rugged.'

He turned his attention to the way ahead. 'Nobody bothers to visit Blunteree because it doesn't have much to offer. There isn't any reasonable beach.' He shrugged. 'Our only ugly island.'

They had almost passed the island when Karen glanced over Miller's shoulder, and blinked. High over the shoreline on the far side of the island she saw the faint outline of a big transparent bird against the sky. She blinked again.

There is no such object, she told herself, as a see-through bird. There just isn't one . . . But when she stared again, carefully and hard, the shape still hovered, a large and definite bird with wings outspread.

It was out of Miller's view because he sat in the stern, gazing ahead, but Karen saw it clearly.

Had it not been for that moment of sun-glitter the shape would surely have remained invisible; but now that she was aware of it, she followed its outline, floating like a piece of cloud-vapour, with fascinated disbelief.

She leaned forward to attract Miller's attention, but something stopped her, an intuition that had nothing to do with logic; and as she watched, the fragile shape dipped and vanished behind the curve of the island. But not before Karen realised this was no real bird at all. It was a child's kite, floating above an island that should have been unoccupied.

She found herself shouting, 'Miller—Miller—stop!'

Eyes comically raised, Miller turned the boat in a wide frothy curve and slowed.

Karen pointed to the isand.

'That one.'

'Blunteree?' he stared at her incredulously. 'It's the roughest of the lot, darling. No decent beach to play on. Why that one?'

She could have told him about the kite right then; he'd given her the perfect oppportunity. But she didn't.

Instead she pleaded, 'Would it be all right if I went there? Oh, Miller, please! I mean—is it a nuisance?'

Miller said, 'Nope, not if you've set your heart on it, dear girl. But you're in for half an hour of utter boredom, darling. There's absolutely nothing to see, and a hell of a climb to the top, trees all around to hide the view. The only beach is covered with pebbles, very hard on the feet.' He was looking again at her thongs, studying her doubtfully. 'However, if that's what you want.' And she begged, 'Oh yes, please, Miller!'

There was a ring of coral around Blunteree, but Miller's small boat skated over it with inches to spare. Once he pointed to a turtle sculling itself through green water in a channel; then to a shoal of blue and silver angel fish; and Karen nodded and smiled, but all the time her mind was asking, Who could be flying a kite on a deserted island? and once she asked herself, And why aren't I telling Miller about it?

He landed her in a small cove with stony sides, its scanty beach covered in pebbles of white quartz polished smooth by multitudes of tides.

A line of pandanus palms stood like grotesque sentinels at the foot of a steep slope. As Karen scrambled out of the boat Miller looked at her severely.

'You're making a mistake, sweetheart. You'll be bored to tears. I'll get back as soon as I can.'

But she was already inspecting the climb behind the pandanus palms, deciding it was negotiable.

'Don't break a leg,' Miller called cheerfully as he headed out across the reef to collect his oysters elsewhere; and she waved at him before she turned to scramble up the slope to the crown of the island.

Miller had been right about the thongs, they were more of a hazard than a help. She took them off and climbed barefoot, collecting dust and a few minor scratches before she reached the top.

She stood and looked around her, at the sea tumbling over the reef below, at the thick and rather forbidding bushland in the centre of the island. She hadn't expected so many trees. On top, the island sloped down into a saucer-like depression covered by more trees and creepers, and she pushed her way through them carefully until she discovered a rocky crevice that gradually widened until it led her, through casuarinas and eucalypts and occasional banksias, to the other side of the island.

Here the land flattened out into a gentle slope, and at the bottom of it she saw the familiar fair-headed figure of Dain Lammont's companion. The curly blonde head was bent, fingers unravelling kite-string, and the kite itself lay nearby, a large bird-shape made of clear plastic.

Karen shouted 'Hello!' and a bird shrieked as it flapped out of a tree beside her, but the person below paid no attention.

She was bending down, replacing her thongs, when a cold voice said, 'It's no use shouting. He can't hear you.'

The voice jerked her upright. Dain Lammont. It was one thing to confront the man in her own territory, but to be discovered before she was prepared set Karen's nerves quivering. Then she steadied herself.

She said illogically, 'Why can't he hear? The wind's blowing that way.'

He, the man had said. Now that was a surprise. Karen had assumed his companion, only dimly seen in half-light as yet, to be a girl. The cool derisive eyes scanned her dishevelled appearance. The hateful voice hadn't lost its irony.

'It doesn't matter which way the wind is blowing. Makes no difference at all. Leon is deaf.'

'Oh!'

That shook her. She studied the grim features doubtfully, searching in vain for any sign of amiability. Then she summoned pride.

'If he's deaf, shouldn't he be somewhere—somewhere safer? What's he doing out here?'

The man gave an exasperated sigh.

'What does it look as if he's doing?

Her confusion deepened.

'He's—he's flying a kite.' And when the man made
no answer she added testily, 'Couldn't he fly it just as
well somewhere else?'

She hadn't expected the question to sound so lame.
She didn't usually ask inane questions, but Dain
Lammont's taciturnity was very off-putting.

'He prefers to fly it here.'

That was her answer, the only one he was prepared
to give. The voice was even grimmer than before,
edged with ice and uninviting; and the man let her
stand there, searching for some kind of retort and failing to find it, before he spoke again.

'Now,' he said bleakly, 'perhaps you'd like to explain
why you're here?'

Karen decided uneasily that of course she ought to
have expected that kind of counter-question. She wished
it didn't make her feel so defensive, even guilty.

She didn't like stickybeaking, and that was exactly
how she probably looked to Dain Lammont, like an
inquisitive female, tracking him to his hideaway, his
lair . . .

'How did you get here?' He was pressing the point.

'I came by boat.'

She veiled her eyes quickly, before he decided to
read her thoughts.

'You really didn't swim out?' His lips twisted. 'That
would have been more appropriate for a mermaid,
wouldn't it?'

They stared at each other silently, then Karen licked
her lips with her tongue and added defiantly, 'Of
course I didn't swim out. I came to have a look. I
mean, I saw the kite flying and Miller said there was
nobody on the island——'

He interjected sharply, 'Miller? Does Miller know
I'm here?'

She replied huffily, 'No, he doesn't. Not yet,' feeling a curious satisfaction to see the tightening muscles around his mouth, a tension in the way he stood, as if she might have slipped beneath his guard.

Then he said softly, 'Not *yet*. I wonder now what you could mean by that comical remark.' And then, with a look of sardonic humour, eyes steel-hard under those dramatic brows, he asked, 'Do I have to do some more persuading?'

Karen took one backwards step.

'No, you certainly don't,' she snapped.

He laughed then, a callous laugh, and Karen's lips tightened. She was dusty, her hair breeze-ruffled, certainly not all that sure of herself; but she didn't intend to be laughed at. She stared at him defiantly, and his eyes narrowed.

'I take it you don't feel any explanation necessary for your intrusion?'

She countered stubbornly, 'I'm free to come here whenever I feel like it. Miller told me these smaller islands are mostly national parks.'

'Mostly.'

'Oh.' She stared at him, bemused. 'You mean——?'

'I mean, you've come barging in where you're not wanted. Could I put it any plainer? Do you usually come visiting without invitation?'

'There aren't any notices up anywhere—at least, I didn't see any.'

Her courage was evaporating, she tried hard not to let him see it, but he wasn't helping any.

'What do you want me to do? Hang up signs "All shipwrecked sailors shot on sight"?' His tone was sarcastic. 'You didn't see any welcome notices out either, did you? Nothing that said, "Climb right on up to the top and have a picnic on somebody else's property"?'

'No, I didn't.' Karen shifted uneasily. 'And you needn't worry. If you don't want anybody to know you're here, I don't see why I should bother to tell them, although I'd like to know what you're up to.'

'I'm not up to anything.' His voice was whiplash-sharp. 'I'm holidaying with my young—er—relative. Minding my own business. If it's any concern of yours. Tell me, do you make a habit of intruding where you aren't wanted?'

He'd touched a sore spot. To her horror, Karen felt her eyes filling with sudden tears.

'Oh yes,' she said, 'I certainly have been doing a lot of that lately.'

She hunched her shoulders, and found no more words to answer his brusque query. An ironic gleam showed in his hard eyes.

'So that's it, is it? Now we have the reason for that woebegone look.' His clever face sharpened. 'Somebody didn't want you. Well, you're not the first person that ever happened to.'

He was quick—too quick. Jumping to conclusions. Karen stared helplessly at his perceptive face, hating him, hating herself for being here.

'All right. I'm sorry I can't get any farther away than the beach until Miller comes back. But I'll sit down there and wait for him, unless you want me to swim away and drown. And if—if you didn't want people visiting, you shouldn't fly that silly kite.'

He didn't point out, as he might reasonably have done, that he wasn't the person flying the kite. He simply raised those flyaway eyebrows and said, 'Ah yes—Leon. I suppose you'd better say hello now you're here.'

He bent and picked up a small stone and bowled it down the slope. His aim was perfect. The stone skittered between boy and kite; the slight figure twisted swiftly, looking up.

Karen saw a happy face, smiling radiantly as if the pebble was the most exciting thing that had ever happened to him.

The boy dropped his string, turned and scrambled up the slope. He smiled at Karen, his face alight with pleasure as he looked from her to Dain Lammont.

Dain directed, 'Tell him your name while he's looking at you. Say it slowly.'

Karen pronounced her name carefully, and the boy studied the shape her lips made.

'Ka—ren.' His voice was husky, his eyes laughed at her with mischief. He pointed to himself. 'Le—on.' And Dain Lammont said with unexpected softening, 'Come on, Ka—ren, let's see if we can find something cool to drink for you two children. How long before Miller comes for you?'

'Not long. He said half an hour from when he dropped me. He's collecting oysters for Jenna.'

As they walked down into the hollow that was the middle of the island, Karen found the ocean disappearing completely from sight. She said anxiously, 'He'll be worried if I'm not there. I wouldn't want to miss him, Mr—er——'

'My name is Dain. You'd better use it.'

A flash of devilry almost had her asking, 'What about the other names you use?' but that would have meant instant termination of her visit. The grim no-nonsense expression he turned towards her as he helped her over a fallen treetrunk made her quite certain of that.

She said, changing the subject, 'How old is Leon?'

'Twelve.'

She paused, surprised. 'I thought he would be older. He's tall for his age, isn't he?'

Dain Lammont looked down at her from his great height. 'We're a tall family,' he answered enigmatically, and from the way he shut his lips deliberately, Karen knew that was all he intended to say.

The boy Leon scampered ahead of them into a casuarina grove, and Karen hesitated.

'May I ask where we're going?'

Dain pushed aside the strands of drooping foliage to let her pass.

'To our island resort, of course. Now you're here, I might as well introduce you. After all, you aren't going to expose us, are you?'

He'd spoken ironically. There wasn't space for a resort among the patch of gumtrees on the other side of the casuarinas. More like a tent, she supposed, sensing the irony behind that terse remark.

But in the bottom of the hollow, shielded from view by a well-placed windbreak of dark green trees, so that you came upon it suddenly with a sense of discovery, Dain Lammont had built himself a wooden hut. It would be difficult to find, unless you knew the way.

Dain Lammont's island retreat was not a sophisticated cabin like those of Wapparaburra. This was a rough structure that looked as if it had been fashioned from driftwood collected on the beach: but it was sturdy and functional, Karen saw as they drew closer.

He pushed open the door into a large room furnished with a rough table, two bunks, a few benches and other pieces of furniture, with what looked like a very small cubicle shut off at one end, protected by a locked door.

The furniture was rough but solid, and he had a decent stove in a niche alongside a makeshift chimney and fireplace.

Dain Lammont must have an obsession about privacy. A padlock and strong chain hung alongside a bolt on the heavy connecting door; obviously this small room was meant to be as well protected as the entrance to the hut, where Karen had already noticed another chain and padlock hanging.

Whatever was in that small isolated room, it was not meant to be accessible to anybody who visited the cabin.

Instinct told her that Dain was noting her careful inspection of the bolted door, and she turned away guiltily.

The man said, 'You can set out drinking mugs while I produce the orange juice. Or would you rather have pineapple? Sorry we don't own any glasses. You'll find biscuits in the jar, and there ought to be cake somewhere. Think you could manage to set the table for afternoon tea, you being the only person here with the appropriate feminine touch?'

So he was setting her to work, distracting her attention from things that shouldn't concern her.

Karen curled her lips and reached for the large china mugs that sat on a shelf beside the stove.

Leon happily pulled down the biscuit jar, merrily conducting a non-productive search for the mythical cake, which failed to turn up, pantomiming his failure with exaggerated shruggings of shoulders, shaking his head as he peered into empty tins, and soon Karen found herself laughing with him.

The boy was expert at communicating with hands and body language, using his expressive face for emphasis. He was a gifted pantomimist, and Karen had no difficulty understanding whatever he wanted to convey.

Once he darted outside to fetch something, and she asked, 'Doesn't he speak very much?'

'Not much. His education has been rather—ah—neglected.' His mouth closed like a trap on that last word, as if it were bitten off in anger. Then the man lifted his shoulders almost imperceptibly, and added in a more controlled voice, 'He'll have speech therapy on the mainland soon, at a special school, and he's a jolly good lip-reader.' He grinned. 'Too good, sometimes.'

He didn't elaborate, and although Karen would have liked to ask more questions she had a feeling the fragile truce between herself and Dain Lammont could be quickly shattered if she displayed too much curiosity.

She said instead, 'He's bright, isn't he?' and the man nodded.

She looked around to find the boy standing in the doorway, studying them both, as if he knew they were talking about him. His face creased in an impish grin that flowed over into sparkling eyes.

Dain had produced orange and pineapple juices, and although he had announcd that the drinks were intended for 'you two children,' he sat with them at the table and drank pineapple with Karen, while Leon poured a generous supply of orange into his mug.

He looked towards Karen and waved one hand in a rocking motion, eyebrows raised in question.

'Did I come by boat?' She guessed his meaning. 'Yes, I did.' She nodded vigorously, and Dain said wryly, 'It's the only way.' Because there was a gleam of amusement in his eyes Karen became daring.

'Next time I may drop in by kite,' she suggested, and an instant aloofness came over his expression so that she thought, 'He doesn't want any next time,' and for some reason a chill seemed to come down on the afternoon, and she shivered.

'Thinking about that unrequited love affair? That was it, wasn't it?' His voice was offhand. 'Are you quite sure you don't want to talk about it? Hasn't the pineapple juice loosened your tongue?'

Now he was being facetious. Karen said huffily, 'No, thanks. Why should I?'

'Sometimes it helps. Might get it out of your system.'

'No,' she repeated slowly. She wanted to add, And if I did talk about it, it wouldn't be to you. Because I'd be needing sympathy . . . a shoulder to cry on, someone with understanding arms to support me because when I think about it I feel like crumpling in a heap on the ground. I wouldn't want your derision. It's shoring up I need, not breaking down. Nor ridicule . . .

She concentrated on drinking her fruit juice, instinctively screening her eyes, lowering long lashes to hide herself from his cool scrutiny; but when she looked up he was staring at her as though he had read every wave of feeling, every betraying quiver of emotion, and rightly interpreted every one.

Then Leon broke the tension. He offered the biscuit plate, giggling because there was only one biscuit left and Karen refused it politely. So the mood was banished, depression blotted out for the moment.

Leon searched for more biscuits, tipping them generously on to the plate, all the time smiling happily.

Leon carried a notepad and ballpoint pen in his shirt pocket, which he showed her proudly. his 'talking pen,' Dain called it, but the boy scarcely needed to use pad and pencil while Karen was there, his gestures were so descriptive.

Sometimes he broke into the sign language of the deaf, fingers flying, and then it was the tall man who lagged behind, miming 'Slow down' with his mouth and shaking his head.

Dain was obviously new to sign language, and Karen wondered how long they had been together, because if they were father and son they could not have been more unlike. The fairheaded boy with his outgoing friendliness, the dark man, reticent and cynical, they seemed almost two different species. Yet there was an elusive similarity, and Karen's instinct told her that some deep feeling existed between them.

Drinks finished, the plate empty of biscuits, Dain Lammont seemed to feel the requirements of hospitality had been satisfied. They never did find the cake; she suspected it had been eaten before she arrived.

Dain pushed back his end of the bench, saying tersely, 'Now we'd better get you back to where your escort can find you,' and although his expression relaxed somewhat as he signalled for Leon to remain in the cabin and clear the table, Karen sensed behind the perfunctory politeness an urgent intention to get her away from the hut before Miller came looking for her.

She followed him meekly. After all, it was his hut; but a warmer reception would have been appreciated. If it hadn't been for Leon's flashing smile as Dain led her away, she felt her visit would have been almost a total loss.

She didn't realise that she had sighed, a long feathering breath of sadness that left her lips drooping, until the man checked his stride and turned around to face her.

'Regular tragedy queen, aren't you?'

The voice was brusque but his lips twitched as he gazed down at the young face, soft lips not quite quivering but oh-so-vulnerable, amber eyes fringed by gold-tipped lashes, close to crying . . .

He reached out a sun-browned hand and touched her cheek with one trailing finger.

'Sure you don't want to talk about that unrequited love?'

'Why should I?'

'I might be able to turn your thoughts in other directions, perhaps.'

'Don't bother.'

He said, even more crisply, 'We all go through it, you know—first love, first disappointment. Mark it down to experience, Golden Hair, like everyone else has to do. You'll survive.' When she said nothing, he added, 'Another few years and you'll look back on the experience with amusement. You'll tell yourself you didn't really know what love was all about. You only thought you knew.'

She thinned her lips at him in disbelief.

'You don't know what you're talking about. Anyway, it isn't true. I made a slight mistake, that's all. Now we'd better get moving again, hadn't we, or you won't get rid of me as fast as you want to.'

He strode ahead of her, following some track that he could detect and she couldn't. Sometimes he halted, carefully holding an overhanging branch that might have swung back and slapped her.

Sometimes, in small clearings, he walked steadily ahead, as if he might be hurrying to reach the pebbled beach before Miller arrived.

But he needn't have worried. They walked through the last clump of casuarinas on top of the cliffs, and looked down at the small cove, and there was nothing to be seen but ocean and rocks and the pandanus palms standing stiffly at the bottom.

It seemed hours ago that she had struggled up this cliff to try and find the kite, and it had brought her nothing but trouble after all. More secrets to keep, more questions to remain unanswered.

Another intrusion: another instance of putting herself in where she wasn't wanted, being led politely but firmly away.

She shivered, and the man said maliciously, 'Got the miseries again, have we? My, but you're really something, you know that. Miss Misery, drooping around——'

'It's those trees.' Karen shrank away from them unhappily. 'I don't like them. They're spooky.'

'They do sound mournful sometimes in the wind.' To her astonishment he offered agreement. She had expected him to be amused by her fancies, but his face was quite serious. 'Casuarinas, the whispering trees. It all depends on your mood, of course. If your spirits are high they can sound delightfully soothing.'

Karen couldn't believe that for a moment. The ghostly wailing of those slender hanging needles in the wind made her skin creep.

She snapped, 'I don't like it here. I don't know how you can stand it.'

He answered grittily, as though she had made him angry.

'You don't really know much about anything, do you? You're so damn sure you're the only one to understand loving and grief and misery. Other people could teach you a lot.'

'I doubt it. I shouldn't think you'd have anything to teach me.'

The words were out before she had time to censor them or consider what effect they might have on a man already feeling irritated, maybe even threatened.

Horrified, she watched the whitening of his lips, the tensing of his lower jaw as if he might have bitten back a flow of words.

Then before she had time to twist away, he reached out and jerked her towards him, gathering her into another of those punishing embraces that had wrought such havoc to her senses that first evening on the beach at Great Keppel.

Only this time it was much worse. He closed his hands over her shoulders, fingers digging in hard so that she wriggled in his grip, trying to wrench herself free. He bore down hard on her, pressing his cupped hands harder still on her shoulders, so that she whimpered a protest, and he eased his grip a little, only a little, before those white, tight lips closed fiercely over hers.

It seemed to last for ever. He kissed her twice, and the second time was a world away from the first because something new had entered into the contact, something exciting and disturbing. There seemed an underlying tenderness in the touch of his hands as he slid them around her waist, under the cotton T-shirt, letting them lie warm on the skin of her back.

This was contact sensation as she had never felt it before.

When the kissing was done he braced himself, his cheek leaning against the softness of her face and then relaxing; and that would have been all, most likely, except that for Karen the encounter had somehow released all her pent-up stress.

All the bitterness and disappointment of the past week thrust against her fragile control and broke it; and she lowered her head and leaned against his shoulder, weeping silently.

Had it not been for the tears sliding down her cheeks she would not have called it weeping. There were no choking sobs, like the grief she had cried into her pillow in the motel at Cairns. This was the breaking of tension; and once the man touched her face with his fingers, then after a while he cupped his hands around her reluctant face, with its tear-streaks, and lifted it so that he saw quite clearly what had happened to her.

He bent his head, and she thought he might have kissed her again, so she shook her own head in a small gesture of negation.

'Don't worry.' His smile was twisted. 'You're safe,' he assured her. She thought his fingers trembled as they slid along her jawline into the silken strands of her hair. 'But I'm not sure how safe *I* am,' he added softly, as he stepped away from her.

He was talking about her silence, of course, wondering whether she might gossip about the hut and the boy with the kite. That would be his meaning.

He wouldn't be thinking about emotions, about the charge of feeling that had leapt from his strong body into hers in that instant when she lost control and let herself lie weeping against him.

She said, struggling for coolness, 'You're one of those men who—who think of love as—as physical experience. I know your type. Anybody can play at that. You don't understand anything about real feelings.'

His lips twisted again.

'As much as you do,' he rasped. His face was pale under the tan. He had been close to losing control himself and he looked shaken.

It had been foolish of her to come here, thrusting herself on him when he wanted seclusion. Of course he'd retaliated. She couldn't blame him.

She pulled farther away from him, taking a long careful breath before she found the strength to say coolly, 'Well, you've had your fun and made quite sure I shan't intrude into your solitude again. That's what you wanted, isn't it? So now you can relax.'

She was twisting her fingers together, almost wringing her hands, and she looked down at them quickly as if they might have betrayed her.

'I shan't be back,' she announced abruptly. 'Not ever.'

And he said nothing at all, but stood gazing after her as she scrambled down the slope.

That was how she left him, a gaunt and silent figure between the casuarina trees as she stumbled on to the beach where Miller would come for her.

Miller would bring sanity. Miller was reassuringly normal. Not some lean, grim-faced, dark-eyed tormenter who brought confusion and self-doubt to undermine what was left of her confidence.

Karen sat on the pebbled beach, waiting, until the wash from Miller's boat rippled over the reef and set the pebbles rattling.

'Find anything?'

She said evasively, 'Next time I'll choose another island,' and he chuckled and teased, 'I told you so!'

She felt guilty about her evasion, wishing she could tell Miller what she had found on Blunteree Island, knowing she must not.

He had two red plastic buckets brimful of oysters and Karen said, 'Jenna will be delighted.'

Her voice sounded high and thin, and Miller glanced at her sharply but said nothing as she settled herself in the bow of the boat, steadying the buckets with her legs because Miller was making a wide, fast sweep over the reef and out on to open sea, and he was in a hurry.

Karen disciplined herself not to gaze too long at the island of Blunteree as they sped away. She didn't want to attract Miller's attention.

She stole a quick look at the dark rocks, and found him looking at her curiously; so after that she dared not look again.

There was, of course, no plastic kite in the sky. The thought filled her with misgivings. She found herself wishing illogically that she had offered Dain Lammont more promises before she left, that she had explained to him how rare a chance had led her to notice the kite in the sky. She didn't like to think Leon might not be allowed to fly his kite again, for fear of discovery.

As they left the island behind she forced herself to look ahead. She had an inexplicable feeling that Dain

Lammont might still be standing there, watching the small boat speed away, doubting whether she would keep her word to remain silent about his island refuge.

She could have reassured him before she left. For the boy, she told herself, for Leon ... She wouldn't like to know she had been responsible for dimming some of the radiance from that bright and trusting face.

When they reached Great Keppel Island and landed near the boatshed, Miller said, 'Well, sweetheart, you're on your own now,' and she stared at him, not comprehending.

He snapped his fingers close to her face and said, 'Wake up!' and she smiled at him apologetically.

'I'm sorry, Miller, truly I am. I didn't understand——'

He nodded.

'In the boat, I mean.'

She frowned as she lifted the buckets on to the sand, being careful not to spill any of Jenna's precious oysters, and Miller said with exaggerated patience, 'Karen, my darling, I'm telling you—you're free to take the boat out by yourself any time from now on, providing you check with me first. You're good enough, quite capable.'

He was looking at her oddly.

'You didn't sniff any magic mushrooms on Blunteree, did you? Find any mind-blowing potions hidden under rocks?'

She laughed and reassured him.

'It's the salt air.' Such an easy lie. 'I'm sorry, Miller, but the sea relaxes me. I guess it's made me dopey. Thank you very much, but I won't ever touch the boat without asking your permission. You've been very kind to me.'

'It's a pleasure, darling.'

Miller wasn't troubled. He readily accepted her explanation that sea-air had set her daydreaming. He wouldn't wonder any more about what she had discovered on Blunteree . . . nor would he waste time investigating its rocky shores.

He grinned goodbye cheerfully as he picked up Jenna's oysters, a bucket in each hand, and tramped across the beach towards the kiosk.

Karen hurried to the valley, white sand kicking up under her thongs as she crossed the beach and went down into the gully, across the rise and down again to Wapparaburra and Madeline.

Madeline had fallen asleep on her bed as she lay reading. Karen slid the open book gently from under her relaxed fingers, pulling the curtains tighter across the windows to keep out light and noise. Then she quietly set about tidying the embroidery Madeline had left on the table.

Madeline had been busy this afternoon. A cushion cover of red and yellow roses lay almost finished beside the workbasket, and Karen rolled it carefully and put it on the divan, rather than disturb Madeline by going again into her room.

Then she wrote a list of what she needed to buy on her next walk to the kiosk, and had almost completed peeling vegetables for the evening meal when she heard movement in Madeline's bedroom.

'Did I wake you?'

'No, my dear, you did not. I've had my ration of sleep for the afternoon, I don't seem to need nearly as much these last couple of days. I have an inbuilt clock that says enough, and when that happens I know I shan't get back to sleep again. I feel a new woman for the moment. Besides, I want to leave some sleeping for tonight.'

Afterwards, Karen was to remember and marvel at

how refreshed Madeline appeared after her sleep. Because it was only a few minutes later that she turned on the radio, saying, 'You don't mind, I hope, Karen? I feel like listening to some music.'

The music was classical, a selection from the *Peer Gynt* suite, and when the last sonorous chord of Grieg's music faded away, Madeline switched off the radio and said testily, '*Solveig's Song*. I do wish they wouldn't play those things about loneliness and autumn leaves decaying. It makes me feel depressed. Ridiculous, I know. I think I might lie down again,' and there was something in her voice, a striving for lightness that didn't quite come off, that sent Karen walking slowly after her.

Madeline managed a wobbly smile.

'That was a mistake,' she admitted, in a low level voice. 'I ought to have remembered, music sometimes shakes my calm—I don't know why. It's quite happy music, really.' Her voice faded to a whisper. 'It stirs something in me, some depth I don't get down to very often, that makes me wonder whether I've missed something in life, and whether I'll ever get a chance to do whatever it is I ought to do before I leave this planet.'

'I think you've probably done your share.'

Anxiously, Karen led her back to bed, tucked the sheet over her, picked up the book Madeline had been reading.

'Would you like me to read to you?'

'Yes, I would. I do have some tablets, anti-depressants, but I don't take them unless I have to. I'd much rather listen to your sweet voice, if you don't mind.'

'Then don't take your tablets yet. How about a cup of tea or one of my fancy milk shakes?'

Madeline managed a wan smile.

'The reading, thank you. I've left a marker in the book.'

But the mystery didn't hold Madeline's attention for long. Her hands were restless, clever tiny fingers picking at the sheet, and the pallor stayed under the skin. Karen coaxed her out of the bedroom into the living quarters of the cabin, gave her warm milk and sat her where she could look out through the glass doors and see not only the gardens but everybody who passed by.

She said suddenly, 'I always intended to visit England after I retired. My forebears came from Cornwall, a place called Penzance. Do you know it, Karen?'

'Not very well. I went walking along the coast once, My parents live in a small country town in Sussex. We have a market square, with some fascinating old pubs and houses, even an old Tudor mansion, with a curse on it. If you go to England, you must visit my parents and have a look at it.'

'That's very kind of you.' Madeline stirred restlessly. 'I just might do that, if I ever get there. Tell me, do the gypsies in their caravans still wander along the English lanes? That's how I think of England—horses plodding along, pulling painted caravans. My grandparents told me stories about them when I was a child.'

'You might be surprised. An uncle of mine, a newspaper reporter, visited a gypsy festival at Appleby some years ago, and he told me lots of the caravans are drawn by motorcar now. There was even a Mercedes among them.'

'So much for romance!'

'Don't worry, there's still plenty for you to see. You'll encounter your horses.'

'Tell me about your little town, Karen.' Madeline closed her eyes, cupping her hands under her chin, her head nodding. She didn't need book-reading now, she needed desperately something to restore her faith in the future that had suddenly become so shaky. She wanted back her belief in the hopes and plans she had had for the years of her retirement.

So Karen described her parents, her girlhood, the woods and the south pond and the museum. The old Tudor mansion, once gutted by fire, now partially restored.

Several times while she talked, Karen thought Madeline might have been drifting asleep, but always when she fell silent Madeline whispered, 'More, please.'

Later she said, 'You're better than any anti-depressants.'

She was still pale, although she managed a gleam of confidence as she said, 'I'm going to make that trip, even if I do have to wait longer than I planned. I'm glad there's so much to see; it keeps me going, knowing it's over there, waiting. All I need is a good report from the doctor next time I go for a check-up.'

Towards the end of the afternoon, most of her depression vanished.

She said, 'It's Friday, isn't it? I thought Victor might have come. I expect he'll arrive tomorrow.'

'Very likely.'

Another weekend, another visit from Victor. Karen would have looked forward to it, except for Madeline's open efforts to promote more than friendship between her nephew and Karen.

Victor was a truly nice person, and nice men, Karen reminded herself, were hard to come by. But all she wanted now was to do her job looking after Madeline as well as she could.

She said now, 'We'll have to wait for tomorrow's boat, or the plane,' but she was wrong.

Madeline settled herself at the table to write another

letter while Karen prepared dinner, when they heard the crunch of footsteps outside, followed by a gentle tap on the door, and Victor called, 'Anybody home?'

Madeline had pulled the curtains while she wrote, now she hurried delightedly to fling them back, her face alight with pleasure.

She cried, 'Come in, do come in,' and led Victor inside.

Victor paused just inside the door to hug his aunt and smile at Karen, before he said, 'I've brought a friend with me, Aunt Madie. Can you and Karen put up with two of us for the weekend, instead of one?'

He stepped aside to allow his companion to come in, and Karen stood frozen, one hand clutching the table as if it were a lifebelt.

Her heart lurched with love and pain and shock. Because the man framed in the doorway, looking so poised, so sure of his welcome—tall and straight and splendid as a perfect lover should be—was Andrew.

CHAPTER FIVE

KAREN stood numbly while Andrew allowed himself to be presented to Madeline, then Victor said, 'I don't have to introduce you, Karen, because you two already know each other.'

Andrew clasped Madeline's hand, complimented her smoothly on the beautiful gown she wore, then he stepped towards Karen and wrapped his warm fingers around her hand and squeezed, as if there had never been any angry words between them, no tragic parting.

Karen had no defence against him. Just as in England he had charmed her into instant devotion, dazzling her so easily that she would have followed him to the centre of the earth had he beckoned, so now he took her yielding fingers and curled his own around them, and gazed down at her as if she were the most beautiful and important thing that had ever entered his world.

But this time Karen knew better than to believe it. Rattled she might be, and far too shattered to control her responses when he looked at her like this; but she had at least learned this one thing: that it wasn't wise to let a man know when he threw you off balance.

Madeline was delighted with Andrew's compliments.

She chuckled, 'A flatterer has come among us,' but she was obviously intrigued, and when she heard Andrew's name she glanced at Karen, smiling delightedly, waiting for her reaction.

They were all watching Karen—Andrew with confidence in his welcome, Madeline and Victor with caring and affection, enjoying her delight at this reunion with an old friend. Karen knew she must not fail them.

She put on a cool face, released her fingers, saying, 'This is a pleasant surprise, Andrew. I certainly didn't expect to see you here.'

The last part at least was true. She certainly hadn't expected him, not after that cold farewell in Cairns.

Andrew lightly kissed her cheek, curving one arm protectively around her shoulders, as if he had never deserted her.

And if Madeline was a little put out that Victor should have brought this undoubted charmer along as competition, just when she was matchmaking for himself and Karen, she soon responded to Andrew's enticements.

She couldn't honestly imagine Victor competing with

his charismatic companion for any girl's attention, but she would wait and see.

Andrew and Victor had rented another cabin. Madeline offered, 'You'll eat with us. We'll be delighted to share with you, if Karen doesn't mind the extra work.'

And Karen lied in her teeth and told them it would be a pleasure to add two extra guests to her schedule for the weekend.

'No trouble at all——'

During dinner, she watched Andrew casting his spell over Madeline, over Victor, over herself . . . so skilfully. For the first time, she found herself making critical judgments of Andrew. He was, she saw, a pleaser, and a practised one. She wondered why she hadn't noticed before.

'Besotted,' she reminded herself. He was weaving his spell around Madeline, making her laugh, dispelling the remnants of her depression. Karen gave him credit for that; but she would be careful in future. Careful with her feelings, careful with her trust.

She would have to be, she decided late that night, clearing away the last of the supper dishes after Victor and Andrew left.

For her own protection . . . because if she was not careful she could find herself back in grief.

Look how easily Dain Lammont had stirred her physically, using his body to shatter calm, and waking unfamiliar sensations that made her uncomfortable. And Andrew so easily took her heart, moving it to breaking simply by using his charm.

Neither man, Karen vowed, would ever again be allowed to guess the effect he had on her. Never again would she be so easy to capture . . .

'If this is growing up,' she told herself later, turning off the light, tucking herself into bed, watching the trees wave outside her window, 'then I don't like it at all!'

Victor called early next morning with an armful of supplies: cereal, eggs and milk, and a large box of meat and vegetables and cooked chicken.

'You aren't staying for six months,' Madeline reminded him, but she sparkled now, and Karen realised what a vibrant woman she must have been before illness depleted her.

Karen was dressed in lime green pirate pants and sleeveless white cotton top that moulded her slender young body; and Victor looked at her for what seemed a long time.

Madeline murmured, 'He's an agreeable young man, Victor. Your friend Andrew, I mean,' and Victor responded enthusiastically.

'Splendid young fellow. He'll soon be a very busy young man, too,' he added cheerfully. 'He's just become engaged to the daughter of one of the wealthiest cane growers in Queensland—a young Italian girl, an only child, so Andrew will be groomed as future manager of the property. It's an enormous responsibility. He'll do very well,' he added approvingly.

If Madeline was delighted to learn that Andrew was already spoken for, she revealed it only by a quick pleased smile. Now she could go ahead with her plans for Victor and Karen.

But Karen stood at the gleaming sink, filling the electric kettle, her knuckles clenched white over the handle as she tried to accept this ultimate betrayal. No wonder Andrew hadn't welcomed her in Cairns! He had his glorious future all mapped out, and she could have ruined it.

How long had he stayed loyal to the promises he

made her? Not long, she decided. He'd warned her he was no letter-writer, and she'd had nothing but the occasional postcard, ambiguous and unrevealing, which should have warned her, now that she thought about them critically; but at the time they had seemed an affirmation of his love, a promise that he still wanted her.

She straightened her shoulders and walked to plug the cord of the kettle into one of the power points. The sound of the kettle singing did nothing to break the ice around her heart.

In a few moments she would have to turn around, letting Madeline and Victor see her face.

'Smile,' she ordered herself firmly. 'You can do it. Smile, and hold up your head as though none of this reaches you. You don't have to drift around looking like a tragedy queen!'

Those were Dain's words, and suddenly she was including the lean dark man with the clever face in the wave of anger that washed over her.

She had been right in what she decided last night; both Dain and Andrew were men who used the means they knew best to get what they wanted. Andrew with his silver tongue, Dain with his powerful body, never condescending to persuade by using compliments or coaxing.

She didn't feel any better when Andrew came for his breakfast dressed in cream tailored shorts and striped casual shirt. He looked spectacular, strolling in the sunlight through the bright gardens.

Male model material, Karen told herself scornfully, angry because her heart leapt crazily, reminding her that the death of one's dreams is totally unacceptable because dreams ought to be for ever.

Yet here she was smiling calmly, prettily, serving breakfast and watching Madeline sparkle as the two men entertained her.

After the last slice of toast, Victor rose to help with coffee, but Karen waved him back. She would keep herself away from the laughter, that was the role for her this morning.

Afterwards, Victor helped with washing up. Andrew wasn't too pleased about that, he had intended it to be his privilege. He offered, 'I'll earn my breakfast and stay with Karen while you two sit outside in the shade,' but Victor claimed the tea-towel and steered Madeline and Andrew into the garden, leaving Andrew no option.

Andrew wasn't a patient man. He came inside several times, commenting pointedly on the time they were taking, and Karen suggested coolly, 'Why don't you and Victor go sunbathing and let me finish?' and he went sulkily outside.

Next time he put his head around the doorway he asked, 'Who's that guy in the cabin next door?' and Victor answered, 'Nobody knows.'

'Unsociable sort of beggar, isn't he? Just stalked by with an icy nod. What kind of bloke behaves like that on holiday?'

'Perhaps he isn't on holiday.' Victor wasn't giving anything away. Maybe he didn't have any information to give.

Karen remembered the dinghy she had seen on the beach the night she arrived; that must be how Dain travelled between his island and Great Keppel . . . To collect mail and provisions, Jenna had said. His letters that came addressed in more than one name . . .

Karen collected the damp tea-towel and some clothing to take to the laundry. Both men looked as if they might have liked to walk with her, but since she was obviously going to do washing, they stayed with Madeline in the garden.

Karen hung her washing on the community clothes-line and walked to the kiosk.

It was time she sent a few postcards, reminders to friends and family telling them what a wonderful time she was having. Her mother wouldn't believe a word of it, of course. Her mother knew full well that Karen had flown out to Australia to join Andrew, a venture she had contemplated with misgiving. Karen was her only daughter, her only child.

Margaret Fallon would quickly note the address. She would also notice with alarm that nowhere in those pseudo-happy little notes would there be any mention of Andrew or of her daughter's impending marriage.

As she entered the kiosk Karen scarcely noticed the tall man standing at one end of the counter, but the fair-haired boy tugged at Dain's arm.

'Ka—ren.' His lips moved carefully. He nodded and chuckled, and Karen waved to him.

The man had a handful of letters, and as he came towards her she involuntarily glanced down at them. The addresses were hidden by his curved fingers.

As if he understood her suspicions, Dain raised those remarkable winged eyebrows even higher, and his thin lips twisted in far-from-polite recognition.

Karen chose her postcards, bought the supplies she needed, and when she walked down the steps to the pathway outside she was astonished to find the man and the boy waiting for her.

Leon perched on the top rail of the fence, watching a kookaburra tugging a worm from the grass. He gestured, laughing, while Dain Lammont stood in the middle of the narrow path, making it impossible for Karen to walk around him.

Dain said mildly, 'Good morning, Karen,' and she looked at him with suspicion. He was going to pretend, then, that yesterday had never happened.

If that was what he wanted, she would do the same. She said good morning, in a stiff little voice, and moved as if to walk around him.

'What's the matter? Not feeling friendly this morning?' His voice was bland.

'Why should I be friendly?'

'Yesterday you drank my pineapple juice,' he reminded her. 'Having accepted my hospitality, I thought you might want to be polite.'

'Not with a serpent.' Karen looked at him severely. 'You haven't been exactly generous with your friendship so far,' she pointed out. 'You must be the most unfriendly visitor on the island.'

'I'm the busiest.' His voice was enigmatic. 'Busy men don't always have time for frivolities. Of course, I could always change my ways.'

'Don't bother.' A little guiltily, Karen turned her face away from Leon, in case the boy was lip-reading. 'Once a serpent, always a serpent,' she quipped stormily.

'Nonsense. Snakes can be be both friendly and fascinating. Try me.'

'No!' she said abruptly. 'Don't waste time trying any more of your tricks on me.'

He looked at her sharply, as if he might be reading something into the vehement protest that she would have preferred him not to see. Then he stood aside and let her walk ahead with Leon, who left his birdwatching to skip beside Karen.

Leon loved the gardens. He darted happily from one to another, pointing out flowers and colours for Karen to see. The fiery-leafed crotons, daubed gold and scarlet; the red star-flowers of poinsettia; creamy frangipanni; he must have seen them countless times, but each was hailed like a new discovery.

They passed a lantana bush, its blossoms almost

hidden in a cloud of black and emerald butterflies. He danced around them with delight, and Karen saw that Dain was prepared to wait patiently until Leon's pleasure was exhausted. It was a new Dain, almost human, gentleness touching his mouth while Leon made soft hissing noises through pursed lips as he admired the butterflies.

In almost every garden there was one tree covered in flowers of buttercup yellow. 'Cassias,' Dain explained, 'also known as Golden Showers.'

Karen glanced at him sideways and he looked at her quickly. 'Also known as . . .' that was the phrase he used so casually. The cassias weren't the only things to have more than one name, but she knew this was not the moment to mention such things.

When they approached the cabins Karen waited to see how Madeline would react when she saw Karen arrive with her unpopular neighbour. Flanked by Andrew and Victor, she was busy with her needlework; she looked up as they approached, her needle suddenly still, and to Karen's surprise Dain and Leon halted, and Karen said lamely, 'We—we met at the kiosk,' because Andrew was scowling and even Victor looked surprised.

Dain had become suddenly polite. He shook hands gravely with Victor and Andrew and introduced Leon, and then he spent some time admiring Madeline's handiwork.

Not smiling, of course, but he was offering more— much more—than his usual bleak good morning, as if suddenly it had become important to him to make their acquaintance.

Only Andrew remained unresponsive. Madeline thawed quickly.

'We should offer you a seat, but I'm afraid we don't have a spare,' she apologised; and the man answered,

'Don't trouble yourself. We're not staying.'

But he did stay. He examined Madeline's work with flattering attention and Karen watched him warily, asking herself what kind of game could he be playing—because there had to be a game. The sudden change in attitude must have some significance.

Madeline smiled at Leon and asked, 'Would you like something to drink?' and Karen went inside and poured drinks, and outside she could hear Victor asking innocently, 'Do you have friends on other parts of the island, Dain? You seem to move about a lot.'

Let's see you get out of that one without telling lies, Karen directed her silent challenge at Dain; but he was expert at protecting his privacy.

'I lead a very busy life,' his voice was unperturbed. 'I've always moved about a great deal.'

'You're not here for the fishing, then?'

Andrew's voice was truculent. He lounged in his chair, refusing to stand and welcome the stranger as Victor had done, and Dain must have felt Andrew's animosity, because his reply was terse.

'Not everybody is here for the fishing.'

Andrew remained noticeably unimpressed. He took little part in the conversation, only interrupting now and then with an awkward question which Dain fended off with discouraging chilliness.

No mention was made of the hut on Blunteree, and with a feeling of sick disappointment Karen asked herself if that was why Dain Lammont had stopped to talk this morning; because he wanted to discover whether she had been gossiping about her visit to his island.

His visit could be an underhand trick, she decided resentfully, carrying her tray of glasses outside.

For a man who didn't smile, Dain captured his audience with great skill. All except Andrew. He talked just enough, saying a lot but telling very little.

Andrew was being childish. He fired his questions at Dain with some belligerence. Where did he come from, what part of Australia? Oh, here and there . . . Nowhere special.

Did he come to Great Keppel often? How long did he stay? . . . That depends. It always depends . . .

The two men were striking sparks off each other, never quite crossing the border from chilly politeness to a flourishing of swords, but they didn't like each other, that was clear.

Madeline raised her brows at Andrew's awkward interruptions. Andrew had obviously let himself get rattled because Karen had walked away from him and returned with the dark man.

It wasn't the kind of situation Andrew liked to be in. He sulked, accepted another cool drink, lapsed into silence.

Karen hadn't realised how touchy Andrew was about little things while they were in England. Now she saw it laid out for her clearly. Andrew didn't like opposition.

All this was in his face as he moved his chair sulkily to a patch of light, and sat watching every move Dain made, weighing every word.

Madeline fussed over Leon, and when Karen brought out slices of cake Dain murmured softly, 'How nice to find somebody who really does have cake!'

If that was a dangerous remark, suggesting a secret shared, nobody appeared to notice.

While Andrew had been polite about Madeline's work, Dain showed a deeper interest, asking whether she had ever considered breaking away from mass-produced designs, producing some of her own.

All of Madeline's embroidery until now had been worked over patterns already stamped on the canvas.

'I saw some canvas pictures and wall hangings in a gallery recently,' Dain told her, 'and I talked with the artist. She sketches her design on to white paper in black ink, then puts her canvas over it and traces the pattern through. It's a fairly easy process, I gather, because of the open weave of the canvas.'

'I'm no artist,' Madeline looked doubtful, 'but I might give it a try, now that I've covered all my friends' dining chairs. And I must say I've produced more than my share of traditional cushions.' She gave Dain a dazzling smile. 'I'll think about it.'

Madeline had come to Wapparaburra for rest and quiet, but the attentions of three attractive men were doing her no harm at all. She had colour in her cheeks, sparkle in her eyes.

When Dain and Leon went to their cabin, she said, 'We really ought to invite them to lunch. I'm sure that man doesn't eat properly, although the boy looks healthy enough. What do you think?'

She was asking Karen. 'Will our provisions stretch?'

Andrew's expression became sulkier, but Victor went across the garden and knocked on Dain's door, Karen saying after him in a small voice, 'He'll probably be busy. He said he's a busy man.'

Nobody heeded, and Victor came back pleased and smiling.

'I told him one o'clock, Aunt Madie. That suit you, Karen?'

No, it didn't suit Karen, but she had no alternative. At least it left her no time for grieving, not a spare second to wonder whether her hard-won cool would crack under the pressure of Andrew's nearness.

She powdered her face, put blusher on her cheeks, folded herself in a large apron and set to work. She made Chinese food—Chicken Chow Mein—an enormous panful; opened tins of ham and asparagus, sliced tomatoes, crisped lettuce to produce platters of savouries and salads.

Leon's eyes brightened as he and Dain sat down, and Dain said drily, 'It isn't exactly what he's used to. I'm only expert at opening tins and boiling eggs.'

Madeline's expression said, I told you so; and Karen remembered how her mother would have reacted to that lean and hungry appearance. She allowed herself to suppose that Dain Lammont knew exactly what effect he was having when he wore that half-starved look. Motherly women were pushovers for under-nourished men, Karen told herself furiously.

And Dain was going out of his way, without losing that high-handed manner of his, to be appreciative, so that Madeline told Karen after he left, 'That's the most delightful meal this cabin has ever produced.'

'It's the company,' Victor said shyly, looking at Karen, flushing slightly, and Karen amended, 'Nonsense! It's the appetites.'

It hadn't been easy, acting placidly, while Andrew's conversation grew grumpier as Dain's became more entertaining; Victor goodnaturedly unaware of undercurrents, his aunt keenly observant, puzzled by Andrew's moodiness but basking in the upward trend her social life was taking for the weekend.

Dain spoke fluently, without emotion. He knew a lot about the Great Barrier Reef, he had visited many of its islands, dived in its waters, and he talked calmly but entertainingly.

When he left, Andrew's poise returned; but Karen realised that for some obscure reason she had felt safe when Dain was there. Her irritation with him was some sort of barrier against Andrew's charm. Now she felt vulnerable again.

Andrew said, 'How about a visit to the resort this afternoon, to the beer garden? You should see it, Karo.

You ought to look at everything while you're here.'

Karen said, 'Not for me, thanks. I've a few things to do,' but Victor accepted warmly. That wasn't exactly the arrangement Andrew had in mind, but he had to go along with it.

So later that afternoon Karen and Madeline sat in the speckled sunlight while Andrew and Victor walked to the resort. Karen remained obstinately determined not to go with them.

'I'm tired,' she lied. 'I need rest.'

Miller came around to set the garden sprays, and plumes of water splashed among the exotic flowers, while the birds called to each other in voices that ranged from sweet to strident.

Madeline lay back in her recliner, closing her eyes.

'No indoor siesta this afternoon. It's too beautiful out here to go to bed.'

Karen worried about the hectic flush on Madeline's cheeks, but she was smiling contentedly.

'Isn't it too blissfully beautiful?'

'Yes, it is.'

'You should have gone with the men, you know, dear. I don't need you here. I've quite recovered from my dive into despair.'

Karen busied herself sorting embroidery cotton. 'I didn't want to go; but thank you.'

Of course, Madeline guessed there were undercurrents; she could hardly fail to notice the thunderclouds on Andrew's face when Dain stayed to lunch, the almost malicious way Dain had made short work of Andrew's efforts to put him down. They did not escape her. She hadn't missed, either, Andrew's rather obvious attempts to get Karen alone, nor Karen's determination not to let him do that. No doubt she guessed there was more to Karen and Andrew's relationship than casual acquaintance, but she would not ask.

Perhaps Madeline understood Karen better than Karen understood herself, feeling quite sure that when the time was right Karen would confide in her why she moved about the cabin with troubled eyes and pale cheeks.

Madeline sighed. She wanted Karen to eat her heart out for Victor, not the good-looking young man who seemed to have a devious reason for visiting Wapparaburra, even if he was safely engaged to somebody else.

Immediately after lunch, Dain and Leon disappeared from the valley. No one saw them go, but the rainbow lorikeets flirted in his banksia tree and drapes covered doors and windows.

Maybe the boy and the man had gone exploring some other part of Great Keppel Island; maybe they were already on their way to Blunteree. Karen stared up at the clear blue sky. A warm wind stirred the trees on top of the ridges. It was a splendid afternoon for flying kites.

She closed her eyes. She could have been almost happy here, if Andrew had kept away. All wounds healed eventually, she knew, so it was reasonable to expect that she might have put together the pieces of her shattered pride and taken up her life again—not without scars—oh no, she would never again be without scars—but she could have survived.

That was what Dain told her on Bluntree: 'You'll survive.'

She was deep in reverie when Madeline sat up suddenly.

'I'm going to work. I mustn't let myself grow lazy.'

She picked up her canvas, threaded the needle and began stitching, all without looking at Karen.

Then she asked suddenly, 'Why don't you try some needlework? I'll give you lessons, if you like.'

Karen shook her head.

'Thanks all the same. I was never any good at it. Simple dressmaking, yes. I can make my own clothes, provided the pattern is simple; but that lovely work you do is quite beyond me.'

'I've been chewing over Dain's suggestion.' Already he was Dain, no longer 'that man.' So easily, without anything you could call a real smile, Dain had won Madeline. Karen couldn't imagine why he'd bothered, but if it gave Madeline pleasure then she was all for it.

'Didn't you approve of Dain's suggestion?' Madeline's eyes twinkled, challenged, watching Karen carefully, and Karen realised she had allowed her suspicions to show.

She said hurriedly, 'Yes, of course. I mean, if it appeals to you,' and Madeline put down her work.

'Yes,' she said firmly. 'He's right, you know. There isn't any need to be confined by other people's designs. I might try a few wall hangings, something typically Australian. I could even add other things to the stitching, glue on some shells and pieces of bark and dried flowers. How about a mixture of embroidery and collage? Or are you a rose lover?'

Karen laughed.

'It sounds ambitious, but why not, if you fancy it.'

'Yes, let's be ambitious. I'll broaden my horizons. What kind of an artist are you, Karen, could you sketch me something?'

'I'm sorry, but to be honest, I've no sense of design or proportion. I'm afraid I'm just one of those who can't.'

'Never mind. You do other things very well. I, too, may be one of those who can't, but I'm jolly well going to try. Remind me to ask Victor to bring drawing paper and black ink on his next visit.'

So Dain Lammont had achieved something. He had supplied Madeline with a new interest, something to help shed depression.

And I, Karen decided firmly, can shed mine . . . She was straightening threads for the yellow roses when she remembered the enchanting carvings on the rotunda in the staff gardens. She could probably copy some of them reasonably enough for Madeline to improve on.

Tomorrow she would consult Jenna and get permission to make a few rough sketches of some of Francis Taupongi's magical creatures.

So here she was, nourishing the seed that Dain had planted. With an exasperated sigh, she pushed away the skeins of thread and walked inside.

She did not see the sudden stillness of Madeline's hands, nor the fleeting half-smile that touched her lips as she watched her slender companion disappear into the cabin.

She had not missed the effect the man from the next-door cabin produced in Karen, the bristling antagonism in young golden eyes as the girl warily observed his behaviour.

Madeline had handled people, been intrigued by their behaviour, all her working life. Their human weaknesses and variable qualities fascinated her.

Now she was aware she had all the makings of a drama to be played around her, right here in the valley, and she didn't intend to miss any of it.

A tiny smile played around her mouth still, as she re-threaded her embroidery needle with crimson thread.

Young love, rose petal red, never to be forgotten. Most of us lose our first love, she remembered, turning back the years as countless lovers had done before her, recalling the first sharp loss.

She pierced one corner of her embroidery, where a fallen leaf lay against a background of lighter green. Beside it she stitched the outline of one red petal, filling it in deftly, soft and velvet-smooth . . . one fallen petal, shaped like a crimson heart.

CHAPTER SIX

DINNER that evening turned into a celebration, because Victor produced several bottles of Madeline's favourite white wine.

Madeline protested, 'What is this? An orgy?'

'No, dear aunt. This is your weekend supply. And what's more, Andy and I are taking you and Karen to the resort tomorrow for dinner. We think Karen deserves a rest from the proverbial hot stove.'

'That's right.' Andrew had mellowed now. He looked magnificent in fawn slacks and white polo sweater. 'We've booked a table for four. All you have to do is be there, Miller will drive us, and enjoy yourselves.'

He was telling Karen, challenging her. A table for four . . . letting her know there was room for no one else, in case she thought of including the man next door.

It didn't matter. Madeline was already planning what to wear, tonight and tomorrow. Victor shrugged and said, 'You're supposed to relax. Don't worry about dazzling us,' but his aunt was determined.

She chose a floating gown splashed in shades of lilac, and Karen brushed her hair and arranged it in an upward sweep, so that when she went into the main room of the cabin Victor beamed and said 'Hello, what have we here . . .?' and even Andrew looked impressed.

Karen retired to her own room. She took out her only formal dress, the garment she had expected to wear with Andrew under very different circumstances, a cool polyester green with full-circle skirt and a halter neck tied with a tiny bow of glittering gold.

When she went inside and would have covered herself with the familiar apron, Victor took it away from her, murmuring, 'Wood nymphs don't belong in kitchens. It's my turn to serve dinner,' and steered her to a chair beside Madeline.

The serving wasn't difficult, because Karen had everything prepared.

They were sitting around the table when Madeline asked, 'How is it you'll be here for the evening meal tomorrow, Victor? Don't the boats leave mid-afternoon?'

'Stroke of luck, Aunt Madie. Les is over again to work on his house, so we can sail back to Yeppoon with him first thing Monday morning.'

Andrew was pouring wine, and Victor asked, 'I take it you won't object to a bit of early-rising Monday morning, Andy?'

Andrew filled Victor's glass, slowly and carefully, not looking at anybody. He took his time, handsome face bent as he concentrated on the pouring.

Then he put the glass beside Victor, saying lightly, 'I've been thinking about that, old chap. About going back, I mean.' His voice very casual . . . 'I don't think I'll leave on Monday, after all.' He tried to make it sound light, tossing it off as if it were not a bombshell. 'Jenna tells me our cabin is available for the rest of the week, so I'll ring home tomorrow and tell them I'm staying longer.'

It could have been an awkward moment. Victor

picked up his glass slowly, staring at the wine. He didn't fancy the idea of leaving Andrew behind when he left, and it showed.

Madeline asked pointedly, 'When is your wedding day, Andrew, have you set the date? You'll have a lot to do in the next few months, won't you?'

She was being protective. She didn't appreciate Andrew hovering around while Victor was away, and she didn't care if he noticed it.

Andrew's voice was defensive as he explained, 'I met a couple of friends at the resort, chaps I went to school with. They want me to keep in touch, so naturally I shan't disturb your peace here very much.'

After that everything went smoothly. Dinner finished, the wine drunk, dishes cleared away, Victor brought out a Monopoly board, and Karen was glad about that because it left little time for anything but light conversation.

Karen watched Madeline for signs of tiredness, but Madeline had no energy problems tonight.

The involvement she had once had with countless pupils had narrowed down, now, to one young girl—Karen. She felt fiercely protective; there was no way Andrew would be allowed to get Karen on her own tonight.

Once, Andrew said, 'Perhaps you'll have time to show me some of the island next week, you two ladies,' and Karen answered quickly, 'I don't think we'll have time.' In case that sounded rude she added, 'Madeline has to rest after all this excitement, and I'll stay around to make sure she doesn't overdo things.'

Victor nodded approvingly, while Madeline said airily, 'Nobody asked me whether I want to rest,' but she smiled at them both, Victor and Karen, with affection.

Karen put down her Monopoly cards. 'How about

taking a short stroll with me when you feel up to it, to look at the rotunda? If you like, I'll try and sketch one or two of the carvings for you to work on.'

It was like a stage conversation to Karen's ears; they were talking for Andrew to listen. But Madeline added serenely, 'That's a good idea. We can practise on ordinary writing paper and pens until Victor brings something more professional. I'll have a look at the carvings on Monday morning.'

Victor groaned, 'More commissions,' pretending to be appalled, but Karen realised with sinking heart that he would be back as soon as he could with pens and paper.

It wasn't that she didn't like him more every day. But intuition told her clearly that Victor was already thinking about her with feelings warmer than she could ever give back to him. He would never excite her as Andrew had done.

Karen thought of the week ahead with misgiving. She didn't look forward to keeping Andrew at arm's length any longer.

The friends he was supposed to have met at the resort could well be fictitious; and unless she offended him deeply there was no way she could go on forever preventing him from reviving old feelings, until she was swallowed up again in the old tangle of emotion.

There could only be one end to that kind of involvement . . . another betrayal . . .

The Monopoly game over, the men left for their cabin, and Karen warmed milk and added a dash of whisky. Madeline put down the book she was reading in bed.

'Silly time of night to be reading.' She nodded wryly at the mystery novel. 'I felt slightly over-wound. This has been my most exhilarating day for a while, so I thought I'd better relax before I tried to sleep.'

Karen picked up the book. 'Shall I read while you drink?'

'Yes, read me a couple of pages, please, Karen.'

Two women, years apart in age and experience, yet they were on the same wavelength tonight. In this small act of sharing, the reading of a book, they had pledged an alliance. Whatever happened tomorrow and all the days after it, Karen knew she was not friendless. If Andrew came seeking cheap thrills, he would find himself dealing with not one determined woman, but two.

And so it proved. The next day slid by pleasantly, innocently, culminating in dinner at the resort, and Karen felt that some of the frozen parts of her emotions melted, so that she felt young again, and carefree.

After the meal, Andrew was surprised to find himself escorting Madeline back to the cabin, after Miller drove them most of the way. He didn't rebel against it. He had a whole week ahead to reinstate himself with the golden girl who was rapidly becoming even more desirable because he couldn't have her.

Outside the cabin Victor said hopefully, 'There's some wine left,' and Madeline didn't hesitate.

'In that case, you may both come in. I'm sure Karen can find something to go with it.'

Karen would have preferred a quick shower and bed, but she sat and let the talk flow around her, and perhaps she had a little too much of Victor's white wine, because when Andrew and Victor went to their cabin she had this weird sensation of floating; and when her head finally rested on the soft cool pillow she let weariness and dizziness flow over her in one great wave that washed her off to sleep.

It was very late when she awoke. The moon hung like a gigantic white ball outside her window, and she reached up to close the curtain and blot out the bright white light. Then she heard the noise on the roof; a scampering like some small night animal or bird that gradually grew louder.

She lay waiting for the intruder to move on, but the scratching sounds went on. The only way to make sure Madeline could sleep in peace was for Karen to go outside and send the disturber away. She thought, about it hazily, half awake, half asleep, until the scampering became almost frenetic, and with a deep sigh she tumbled out of bed and crept outside.

The moonlight was like a silver wash over the garden. A tiny dark figure leaped from the cabin roof, over Karen's shoulder, into a tree, and she felt herself silently scream.

Then sanity returned, and she found herself peering at a small possum clinging to a treetrunk. He stared at her with bulbous eyes, out of a plaintive little face, and she felt a ripple of laughter replace fear.

'Terror in the night,' she whispered. 'Do you know you're a nuisance?'

The small creature shifted as if he might leap on to the roof again, and she went quickly inside and collected a handful of sweet biscuits.

'I don't know whether this is possum food or not,' she whispered. 'But here you are. All you have to do is come away from the cabin and you can have it.'

She held out her hand, with a biscuit in it, and a low whisper, quiet as her own, said, 'Beware those claws——'

'Oh!' Karen took a hasty step backwards. 'You startled me!' she said accusingly to the mysterious figure of Dain Lammont, half hidden among the garden trees. 'Would he really——?'

Dain's voice was dry. 'Possums aren't entirely defenceless. Those claws can inflict nasty wounds on an enemy.'

'I'm not his enemy.'

'No.' A slight smile showed white in the moonlight. 'I think he's discovered that already. How many biscuits has he eaten?'

'None yet.' She lowered her voice. 'He was scrabbling around on the roof and I thought he might disturb Madeline. I'm trying to lure him away.'

'Hold your offering out a bit, so he clings to the tree with his paws, and he'll take your titbit in his mouth. Don't you have any bananas? They're a real possum delicacy.'

'No, I don't. Biscuits are all he'll get at this time of the night.'

The possum took Karen's biscuit with his mouth, then settled himself on a branch, holding the biscuit human-fashion between his front paws.

Karen laughed softly, and the man stepped tentatively out of the shadows.

'Noisy eater, isn't he?'

'It's a noisy biscuit, I'm afraid. I should have known he'd have to crunch.'

'Madeline asleep?'

'Yes.'

'How is she, after your hectic weekend?'

Karen didn't ask him how he knew their weekend had been all hectic. She said, 'I believe it's done her good.'

'And has it done you good?'

She stared at him solemnly, lips slightly parted, as if she asked a silent question. Then she made a little helpless gesture.

'Oh, I suppose so. Yes, it has.'

He was being extremely friendly, even gentle, and Karen began to think, how could she ever have considered him a menace . . . He actually smiled. He was very attractive when he smiled, especially with the moonlight gleaming on his face, softening its harsh lines. She hadn't seen him so relaxed before.

Then she glanced down at herself, remembering with a shock that she had got out of bed without thinking about any covering, because the night was mild.

She said confusedly, 'Oh dear, I'm not dressed!' and his eyebrows went flyaway, as if he were secretly laughing.

'I shouldn't worry. I don't think he noticed.' He meant the possum; he was being facetious, and she glared at him indignantly.

'You're fairly well covered, aren't you?' he added, straight-faced. His comment sounded faintly amused, but he backed out of the bright white light, so that he was screened among tree-shadows, as if he guessed that now she was selfconscious because he was a man and she was clad only in a sprigged cotton shortie nightdress that didn't cover very much at all.

Karen had thought, when she put it on, that it made her look long-legged and faintly boyish, but the tiny shoulderstraps and scoop neckline didn't hide very much, and she was suddenly, unaccountably, shy.

She made a sudden movement with her hands, then let them fall limply to her sides. She wouldn't give any man the satisfaction of admitting her embarrassment, especially this cool one.

A bikini on the beach would be more revealing but somehow in this atmosphere of half-lights and moon shadows, perfumed flowers and ghostly trees, everything seemed exaggerated; and she felt naked.

She was hesitating, debating whether it would be undignified to retreat inside, when the possum came down from his tree and shuffled across the garden towards her. She held her breath as he sniffed curiously around her bare feet, whiskers brushing skin as he explored her toes.

'You'd better look out.' Dain's voice quivered with laughter. 'He might fancy you for dessert.'

Hastily Karen tossed her handful of biscuits into the bushland across the path. The possum scampered after them, and disappeared.

The man in the shadows had undergone a quick change of mood. He wasn't laughing now. There was intensity in the way he looked at her, a concentration that made her skin come suddenly alive and tingling, as if he had made some kind of emotional contact with it . . . touching but not touching . . . stirring without contact.

He spoke softly.

'Now there's only us,' he murmured, and something in his voice made Karen's heart beat with a wild kind of exhilaration so that she thought he might see its frantic throbbing under the light cotton garment. Yet she could not move.

She had been correct in her first assessment: Dain Lammont was a dangerous man. He stood there staring at her now like some kind of hypnotist, holding her there against her will, and the feeling between them grew and grew until for her it almost turned into a sound, like a beating of wings in the darkness.

Then she made a superhuman effort, and wet her lips with the tip of her tongue.

She hissed, 'If you come any closer, I'll call Madeline!' and he laughed. Only this time his laughter wasn't amused at all, it was ironic and cruel, and she flinched because she knew it was directed at her, making her feel foolish and gauche, and she knew she ought not to have said what she had said to him.

Then, surprisingly, as if he might have felt sorry for her, he said gently, 'You don't have to call anybody. Why don't you go inside and get back to sleep? Your possum friend seems to have taken himself off somewhere.'

That was true. Karen stared into the darkness, but the possum had collected his biscuits and vanished. When she looked back, she saw that Dain had moved away, too. He was crossing the small courtyard outside his own cabin. Dreamily, she watched him go. She imagined he might have raised one arm in silent farewell, but it was difficult to be sure.

Perhaps he had collected something from the drying line strung outside, or even moved the curtains behind his door; but he did not turn on the cabin lights and Karen knew she would not see him again that night.

She brushed her fingers lightly to get rid of biscuit crumbs. Then she crept inside, feeling her way in the moon's white light.

Because the air was warm she pulled only the sheet over her body, and lay once again listening for any sounds of life outside, but there was only silence.

She was beset by strange feelings of disquiet, as though the day had finished without something being done that should have been done, as if some promise had been unfulfilled.

Karen sighed. Earlier she had been so relaxed, so ready for sleep. Now she lay there, asking herself whether she had been foolish to obstinately refuse to listen to Andrew, whether she was asking too much of life to expect that an experience should be perfect in every way, working out exactly as you hoped it would, instead of falling short and fraught with bitter disappointment, like her relationship with Andrew.

He would be willing to offer her some kind of affectionate friendship. He proved that by being here. Was it better than nothing? she asked herself in anguish.

Andrew. Daringly, weakly, she shaped his name with her lips and her heart gave a lurch of pain. Before she knew it, there were tears soaking her pillow. Too much wine, she told herself fiercely. Too much wine, and too much stirring by the impossible man next door who was so physical it made you shiver.

Who but Dain Lammont would have a presence so powerful that even after he disappeared inside his cabin, there had remained in the garden a suggestion of his presence so potent that she had turned to look for him as she closed the door behind her?

Andrew was less complex, she knew that now. He had his share of human frailties, but when Andrew spoke he revealed Andrew, not an enigma. He mightn't be perfect, but if he had loved her, she would have accepted him just as he was. It was Andrew, she told herself fiercely, who had taught her the feelings of love. Real feelings . . .

So why, then, as she rubbed the tears from her eyes and stared at the moonlight flickering on her wall, why was it that she saw in her mind not the clear-cut fine features of Andrew, but the haunted, hollowed face of the man from the next cabin?

CHAPTER SEVEN

The next day dawned with drizzling rain. Karen hoped it was not an omen. She had finished with tears. Last night's weeping, she promised herself, had been her last surrender.

Sure enough, breakfast over and Madeline ready for her morning walk to the kiosk, the day turned fine again, and the valley sparkled.

Karen walked with Madeline to the kiosk. Jenna's cleaning trolley stood at the bottom of the steps and inside the kiosk Jenna talked to Gracie behind the counter.

She said, 'Hi! You just missed your neighbour, Mr Lammont,' and Gracie chuckled and added, 'Came and went in his usual lightning visit. In, out, and away!'

Madeline's voice was carefully innocent. 'Where does he go when he disappears, does anybody know?' and Jenna shook her head.

'Funny thing, though. There were two men here yesterday asking about him. At least, I think they meant Dain. Tall dark feller, they said, very thin, black eyes and dark hair. Unhappy-looking guy.'

'Official-looking men, they were, and one had a camera. When they thought I couldn't hear one said to the other, "He could be using an alias. He often does." Anyway, when they asked me I said they'd have to see the management, and sent them to the office, and that was the last I saw of them.'

'That's an odd sort of thing to happen.'

Karen saw the gleam of interest in Madeline's eyes, and when they moved to the postcard stand she whispered, 'You should know me by now, Karen—always looking for drama. If there's anything happening I like to know about it.'

She looked cheerfully unrepentant about her curiosity and Karen laughed.

'You won't get much satisfaction out of Dain. He's not likely to confide in us.'

Karen purchased souvenir tea-towels for her mother and postcards to send Melanie and Linda in Canada, and Jenna called, 'Are you walking my way? I've got new people moving into one of the cabins this morning.'

Madeline said yes, although Karen knew she had more shopping to do. But Madeline scented news and she wasn't going to miss out on it.

As they set off with Jenna she enquired shamelessly,

'What other names does Mr Lammont use, Jenna?' but Jenna was being careful.

'Oh, just any old thing. I think he does it for a joke. You know, Smith, Jones, Robinson——'

So Dain Lammont wasn't in any real danger from Jenna. She wouldn't give him away. But was he in any real danger at all?

Maybe, Karen told herself, it was only a whim, this use of false names to protect his privacy.

Anyway, he wouldn't be caught today. His cabin was deserted. He must have made his purchases and moved on.

Madeline went inside and as Jenna prepared to take her trolley further, Karen found herself asking, against her better judgment but because she needed to know, 'Did you tell Dain about the men who were searching for him?' and Jenna looked at her sharply.

'No, I didn't; but someone else probably did. I mean, I sent those men to the office, so I guess somebody there might have passed on the news to Dain.'

But Jenna couldn't be sure, Karen knew, and deep in her mind, some place where reason turned to intuition, she felt a faint pricking of anxiety.

She had no business worrying over Dain Lammont. So perhaps it was for the young deaf boy she felt so concerned, since it couldn't be for the saturnine man who defended himself inflexibly against intrusion by his neighbours.

It was later in the morning when Karen coaxed Madeline into taking the short walk to look at the rotunda. Madeline was delighted with the carvings. She chose several that interested her, and while she sat on a garden bench Karen tried to make rough sketches of those creatures that had taken Madeline's fancy.

There was no way she could repeat the skill of the carver; but Karen made rough outlines that might serve as some kind of basis for Madeline's designs.

Practice made her fingers more flexible; she let her imagination go on the snake, drawing the creature poised to strike, threatening. Then she got to work on the crocodile, turning him into a villain, wondering how Madeline would react when she found those two wild drawings among the placid outlines.

Back at their cabin the four young boys waited with a tray bearing two gigantic fish decorated with hibiscus and silver foil; and Madeline said in a curious voice, 'Red Emperors—how delicious! But you'll have Miller after you if he finds you stealing his flowers to pretty-up dead fish.'

The boys exchanged glances, staring hopefully at Karen, and one of them suggested, 'Any time you'd like to join us——' but Karen shook her head.

'Not for me, thank you. I'm a clumsy lady with fish-hooks.'

She took the fish inside and gave the boys back their tray; and after they left Madeline pursed her lips.

'I can see we're going to have never a dull moment while you're here. Was it this way at home?'

'Which way?'

'All the young man gathering like bees around blossoms.'

Karen stared at her in astonishment.

'They came to bring you the fish!' and Madeline chuckled.

'Up to date,' she confided, 'all offerings have arrived wrapped in newspaper, handed through the doorway with a hasty Good morning, ma'am, we thought you might like a fin or two . . . Now we have a ceremony like the opening of Parliament. Even the mysterious Mr Lammont has softened. Do you always have this effect on the males around you?'

Karen laughed. It was genuine laughter, sheer

astonishment that anyone fancied her in the role of glamour girl, instead of the defeated young woman who had arrived on Great Keppel.

She put the Red Emperor fish in the refrigerator, squatting on the floor as she rearranged the shelves.

'I'll let you into a secret,' she confessed. 'This is almost the first time anyone has bothered to pay me any attention. The boys at school all went for a dashing brunette with beautiful blue eyes. They were bowled over. She had this wonderful throaty voice, and she knew how to flap her eyelashes to distraction. Wow! How I used to envy Chrissy Johnstone. Even after I grew up and went to London, I didn't exactly bowl anyone over. Andrew was my first . . .'

It had slipped out . . .

The cabin became suddenly quiet, and Karen heard a bird outside utter one clear note and after that there was no other sound at all for several heartbeats, until Madeline spoke again.

'Karen, did you know Andrew was coming to Great Keppel Island? Was that the arrangement?'

'Oh no.' Karen shook her head vigorously. 'No. We said g-goodbye.' She swallowed, trying to ease the lump in her throat and failing . . . trying to stop her lips from trembling . . . failing that, too.

'I came here to look after you. Honestly.' She drew a deep breath. 'Andrew and I met in London, when he visited friends of mine. He asked me—at least, I thought he asked me—to come and see him in Australia. So I—I came, and it seems I—was mistaken. So he found this job for me. But if you want me to go,' she added valiantly, 'I'll find somewhere else to work. Or I can fly home.' She stood up, moving stiffly, restlessly. 'You must think me naïve, but I hadn't much experience with men, you see. I just—believed everything Andrew said to me. I suppose I was over-eager.'

Her lips drooped. 'It must have been a bit of a shock for Andrew, when I took everything he said so literally.'

Madeline's face set into sternness, as if she were headmistress questioning pupil, almost accusing.

'But you won't make that mistake again?'

'Oh no.' A bitter laugh. 'That's one lesson I've learned. From now on, I sprinkle a large dose of doubt on everything before I swallow.'

Madeline played with the sketches they had done in the garden, riffling them with her fingers.

She asked suddenly, 'You're not pregnant?'

Karen's face flushed. 'Certainly not!' She swallowed convulsively. 'There never was—anything like that.'

'You must forgive me.' Madeline's voice grew gentler. 'I've seen so many silly young girls. Some of them, of course, the strong ones, they pick up the pieces; but it's the others I'm sorry for, the losers who never quite get back their innocence.'

Karen said steadily, 'I'm not pregnant, nor likely to be, so don't waste your sympathy on me.' Even to her own ears, her voice sounded hysterical. 'I've been stupid, but not that silly.'

'Well, don't let it turn you into Miss Vinegar Puss. That would be a shame.' Madeline's expression softened. 'You understand, I have to ask these questions. I have to be sure I'm not abetting you and Andrew in some shabby little scheme to cheat on his marriage. Andrew was—is—Victor's friend, his family is known to Victor, and I wouldn't want to put my nephew in the position of seeming to betray any kind of trust.'

Karen was suddenly angry. That Madeline should think this of her seemed unbelievable. Yet with a flash of honesty, she knew that was how it must seem to an onlooker, that she had made some sort of assignation with Andrew to meet on the island, using her job with Madeline as cover-up. If only he had kept away!

She said formally, 'I'm sure you can find someone to take my place without too much delay. It shouldn't be difficult.'

Madeline's expression relaxed from cool disapproval into delighted warmth.

'Oh, sit down, my dear, and accept my apologies. I wouldn't part with you for all the treasure on the *Titanic*, if there happened to be any. You've made me feel alive again. If I sent you away I'd deprive myself. You understand I had to be sure, for Victor's sake.'

When Karen didn't move she stood up and reached out and folded Karen in her arms, with their bright floating sleeves, and Karen felt the warmth, the sheer affection of her embrace.

When she let Karen go, Madeline said, 'Now we have to do some thinking, haven't we? What shall we do about Master Andrew? He isn't going to be easily put off. You're a beautiful young woman, even if you don't know it, and I think that young man is only too aware of the impression he's making on you.'

Karen's astonishment was quite spontaneous. She laughed—a wobbly laugh, but it was still laughter.

'Me, beautiful? You must be looking through rose-coloured bifocals!'

But Karen was enchanting, Madeline decided, watching the girl with eyes that speculated while they approved. Probably she had not, as yet, realised the appeal of her delicate heart-shaped face, shining amber eyes shielded by gold-tipped dark lashes, hair like yellow silk and soft sweet mouth.

A slender, sunshine girl, Madeline decided wistfully. Born for cherishing, for desiring . . . Andrew had been only the beginning, although Karen didn't know that yet.

Madeline sighed. Don't interfere, she instructed herself.

But when she heard footsteps, and Andrew's voice called, 'Hello! You're home, I hope,' she muttered viciously, 'I'd like to strangle you!' and her small clever hands tingled as if she might indeed have allowed them the pleasure of closing around Andrew's neck. Then she handed the sketches to Karen and rose to her feet, motioning Karen into her own room.

Don't interfere, she had ordered herself, but Madeline could no more refrain from intervention than she could halt her own breathing.

She greeted Andrew with enthusiasm.

'Come in! You're just the man I want to see. Would you hold some wool while I wind? Karen's busy, doing some drawings for me.'

'I thought it came already wound.' Andrew waved at the skeins on the table.

'Not this lot.'

Madeline sailed into her bedroom and rummaged, returning a few minutes later with a heap of twisted wool. Karen, listening, felt a sudden wild desire to laugh.

She wouldn't be at all surprised if Madeline had spent those vital few moments in her room deliberately tangling wool; and as Madeline settled the threads around Andrew's fingers Karen walked in carrying her sketches, saying calmly, 'Cup of tea or coffee?' and Andrew said yes, thank you, that was an excellent idea. His face was glum; he didn't fancy himself in this domestic role.

Karen was asking herself how they would avoid inviting Andrew to lunch when he said, 'I came to see if you'll come on a hike after lunch. I'm eating at the resort with my mates, and there's some sort of walking tour organised, if you feel up to it.'

'I'm sorry,' Karen rattled cups and saucers, 'I don't

think I could leave Madeline this afternoon.'

Then to her surprise Madeline put down the wool. 'I think you ought to go, Karen. The sketches will keep until tomorrow.'

Afterwards, Andrew left, saying he would meet her outside the resort, and Karen challenged Madeline, 'Whose side are you on?'

'Yours. I'm an interfering old woman, and I can only plead real concern for you. I suppose I've become maternal—even matriarchal—with my girls at college, and I was impertinent enough to carry that attitude over to you.'

'I don't consider you impertinent.'

'Oh, but I am, my dear.' Madeline's voice softened. 'You're a woman, not a child, and quite capable of handling your own affairs. I know you will deal with Andrew very well. I hope our association will continue for quite a while longer, so I don't propose to—er—shove my oar in, I believe my girls called it—when there's no need for it. Anyway,' she added briskly, 'you should see something of the island while you're here. So go on this excursion, and if you clear up a few things with your—your erstwhile young man—then it's all for the better, isn't it?'

However, Madeline proved over-optimistic. The trip was well organised. They were escorted to a long stretch of silver beach where they swam, sunbathed or played badminton on the sand.

Andrew, Karen deduced, must have been slightly offended by her lack of eagerness to accept his invitation. He played it cool, making no attempt to detach himself from the party. In fact, he seemed to rather enjoy basking in the undisguised devotion of several teenage bathing beauties who dogged his footsteps all afternoon.

See, he was telling Karen, you're not the only one

. . . So when they reached Wapparaburra on their return they were pleasantly relaxed, and there had been no heart-to-heart discussion between them. Madeline would be disappointed.

As they turned on to the access track, under the umbrella of a spreading poinciana, Karen made a final effort.

She said, 'Andrew, this has been a very pleasant experience, but——'

And he interrupted plaintively, 'If you've enjoyed it, you might try giving me a warmer welcome next time I call. I'm only here a few more days.'

He was returning to the resort to dine with friends, and he had become very distant because Karen wouldn't join them. The guests at the resort were fancy-dressing in grass skirts and hula tops and coloured leis for a Hawaiian Night, and when Karen resisted he added crossly, 'You could take time off from Madeline, if you really wanted to. She'll do anything for you. You just don't want to come.'

He didn't believe that, of course; that she didn't want to come. Not for an instant. He was so sure of her that he hadn't thought twice about being standoffish all afternoon, so she would re-think carefully before she offended in future.

Now he stared at her with accusing eyes and Karen felt her heart twist guiltily. She steeled herself.

'Andrew, what are you doing here at Wapparaburra?' So easily she pronounced the name that not long ago had tripped her tongue: Wapparaburra. Not so easily could she harden her heart against the hurt expression on Andrew's face. 'Why did you come?'

'What am I doing?' His injured expression deepened. 'You know darned well what I'm doing. I'm here to see you, aren't I? To—to make sure you're all right.'

Karen kept tight hold on her emotions.

'Okay. So now you know I'm all right, you won't have to stay around any more, will you?' She faced him, eyes too brilliant, body defensive. 'Mission accomplished.' Her voice squeaked as if she had asked too much of it, but Andrew wasn't worrying about how she felt. His temper was connected to a very short fuse. He blew it now.

'Don't be so damned ridiculous, girl! We're still friends, aren't we? You haven't stopped caring, neither have I. So I'm making a convenience marriage. What the hell difference does that little bit of paper make? It's our relationship that counts, what we make of it. Not—not conventions.'

The sun shone all around them, and a bird swung on a flower beside the path. It should have been Paradise. Karen wet dry lips with the tip of her tongue.

'How can you talk like that when you're engaged to marry somebody else?'

He was astounded.

'You don't listen, do you? So I'm engaged! What has that to do with—with friendships? My marriage is a family arrangement, it's something that just—just worked out——'

He was uncomfortable, though. He ran a hand through his hair and Karen saw the strands rise and fall under his fingers.

He was splendid and weak, magnificent and devious, and her heart said quite clearly, 'So this is what they mean by feet of clay!'

His glance was evasive.

'Are you trying to tell me that suddenly I'm not allowed any other friendships, any other feelings? We had something pretty special, back there in England. You can't deny that. It brought you out here, didn't it?

All loving doesn't end in marriage. Only in books——'
With Karen staring at him, wordless, he went on,
'You'll never know what it did to me, Karen, seeing
you standing there in the airport at Cairns, telling
myself I wouldn't ever see you again. I went home and
you were in my mind, and there were things I kept
remembering . . .'

Things I kept remembering . . . Karen turned on
him furiously.

'I'm not interested in becoming your—your under-
cover acquaintance.' Her voice broke. 'You fancy
having me on the sidelines, don't you? You . . . you
let me travel out here, believing you still wanted me.
You could have told me, you ought to have written
and explained. Why didn't you? You didn't say anything about sharing your affections when we made
plans——'

She turned away, choking, knowing that if she said
more she would find the words turning sour in her
throat, and Andrew would know how much she cared,
how he could still hurt her.

There was one thing she had to ask, and she did it
now.

'Unless you plan to break your engagement?'

He turned his head, and when he looked back at her
his expression was stubborn.

'I'll do what I have to do.'

'For your family's sake?' she taunted.

'Yes, for my family.'

Perhaps he believed it, that he was marrying not for
his own profit but because his family desired it. But
with her new insight Karen knew that Andrew could
not relinquish his golden future for a little English
nobody.

She turned on her heel, almost running down the
slope towards the valley, but Andrew ran faster. He

caught her and swung her around to face him, and she
was astonished to see his eyes moist with unshed tears,
his lips white and strained.

'You don't believe it, but you'll always be my sweet
and gentle English lily,' he said huskily, and she felt
the tears in her own eyes as she stared at him.

What might have happened then could have spelt
disaster for Karen, except that a figure emerged from
beside the path, pushing aside the yellow banksia
brushes like golden candles against the sky, stepping
out of the reflections that sun and green-cool had made
around its spiky foliage.

It was Dain Lammont, taking a short cut——

If he overheard Andrew's impassioned declaration,
he gave no sign. Ironic eyebrows raised, he nodded
slightly, but when Andrew stood aside to let him pass,
Dain shook his head.

'I'm going your way.'

So that was how the encounter ended, with all three
of them walking to where Madeline sat in the speckled
sunlight of the patio, studying Karen's drawings, looking up as they approached, so there was no excuse for
Andrew to avoid going directly to the cabin.

But his fingers closed on Karen's arm as if he would
never let go, and Dain was forced to walk behind them,
commenting mildly about the weather, neither sneering
nor smiling, but slightly aloof. Karen wondered
furiously why he hadn't continued on his way and left
them to finish their conversation.

Not, she discovered suddenly, that she really
wanted to go on with it, not the way it looked like
going . . .

There were alarm splashes of hectic colour in
Madeline's cheeks, but she looked up and greeted
them, and said to Dain, 'We thought you'd left us.
This morning——'

He interrupted smoothly, 'I forgot something. Had to come back for it.'

He was looking at Madeline, narrow-eyed, and Karen put out one hand and rested it on Madeline's hot forehead, and Madeline joked and said, 'You're very smart, aren't you? But don't worry, I'm not having a relapse. It's just that—Victor rang while you were away, and he's coming to collect me tomorrow, because my medical check-up has been brought forward. Dr Brown has to go to America next week to a conference.'

'You're worried.'

'Just a little. Overdose of apprehension, that's all.' She spread out her hands in apology. 'My future depends on it, you see.' She was explaining more to Dain than to Andrew. 'Now I shall find out whether I've healed as I should have, or whether I must have a second operation. The doctor doesn't expect any complications. Not really.'

Her voice was a little desperate, and Dain said coolly, 'Of course not. Why should they?'

Karen saw that his calm assumption that everything would be all right had acted as some kind of brake on Madeline's panic. A steadier . . .

She added, more to Dain than anybody, 'I've taken your advice. I'm planning to branch out. Would you like to see what we've been doing?' and her hand shook a little as she pushed the sketches across the table; but she was putting herself together now.

Andrew didn't care for Karen's two wild drawings. He looked slightly shocked.

He said uneasily, 'They don't look like your work, Karen. They're not what I'd have expected of you,' his voice almost reproving.

Andrew didn't like leaving while Dain stayed there, but he hadn't any choice, because his friends were waiting. He said goodbye and stalked away, stiff-backed and offended, because Karen made no move to stop him.

For some obscure reason, she would have preferred to screen her wild sketches from the piercing eyes of the man who now picked them up, but it was not to be.

She couldn't think why she felt embarrassed. She hadn't pretended to be an artist. Madeline needed ideas and she had tried to help, fully conscious of her inadequacies.

Dain took a considerable time over the sketches, turning them over one by one, and Karen was disconcerted to find a gleam of amusement in his eyes. He indicated the striking serpent.

'Got rid of a lot of hostility there, didn't you?' He shuffled the pictures. 'What happened? Did you spend the night having bad dreams after your weekend celebrations?'

And when Madeline went inside to look for something she wanted, he murmured softly, 'You're nobody's meek and mild little English lily, are you, Karen?' and there was something in his eyes that she had never seen before, a kind of derision mingled with sternness.

So he had overheard Andrew's passionate persuasion and didn't approve.

She said quickly, 'I have to go. Madeline needs me,' and snatched the sketches out of his hand, knowing it was unmannerly but knowing, too, that she wanted to get away from that searching look that was making her uneasy.

Dain said softly, 'I, too, have to go,' and she understood he was telling her about his island, reminding her of something elusive that she didn't understand.

She said spitefully, 'Ah yes, you're a very busy man, aren't you?' and he agreed, 'I am indeed. Wish

Madeline well for me, won't you?' and with a mocking half-bow, was gone.

Karen found Madeline tense, strung up by the prospect of tomorrow's journey. She packed her overnight bag, unpacked it, packed it again. Then she led her gently to the divan and sat her down, staying beside her, holding her hand as she might have held a child's hand.

'Do you want me to come with you tomorrow?'

'No. I'll have Victor.' Madeline squeezed Karen's fingers gratefully. 'He's coming on the morning boat, and I'll fly back with him on the midday plane. I'm to stay overnight at Rockhampton and come back next day. He's taken some extra time off work—Victor, I mean—so he can travel back with me. He says—I might need him.'

If the news isn't good . . . those words were unspoken, but they were understood.

'I've been lucky.' Again Madeline squeezed the fingers in hers thankfully. 'Fortunate in my friends, ever so lucky to have Victor. Dr Brown has told both of us there's only a remote chance of anything more having to be done. It's just that—my imagination seems to be galloping away with me.'

Karen gave Madeline two sleeping tablets and half a glass of water before she went to bed that night, and much to her surprise Madeline slept peacefully all night.

Several times Karen crept into her room, but each time she found Madeline deep in sleep.

Next morning Madeline had her nervous reactions well under control. Pale but calm, she kissed Victor when he arrived, and by the time Miller called to say the jeep waited to drive them to the airstrip, Madeline wore a cloak of outward serenity that would have deceived all but those who knew her best.

Now, Karen saw how much and how deeply she depended on the calm, gentle nephew who smoothed away her apprehensions with a touch, a light word, a comforting glance.

At the airstrip, as they watched the bush pilot's plane land with its incoming passengers, luggage and supplies, Victor asked Karen softly, 'Did my aunt tell you I've taken time off and I'll come back with her? You understand, it's not because I lack faith in you. It's because—if anything unexpected shows up in this medical, I want to be close by.'

'Would you prefer to sleep in the cabin? Perhaps I could move out——'

He was horrified. 'Never! That wasn't what I had in mind at all. I'll stay with Les. I only want to be around if Aunt Madie needs me. Close enough to give her a pep talk when you run out of breath.'

He wanted so much to be sure Karen's feelings weren't hurt.

She said gratefully, 'I offered to go over with her, but she's certain you'll give her all the support she needs, and I know you will. I'll have a meal waiting tomorrow when you get back.'

That was all she could do, apart from a few light jobs that awaited her back at the cabin. A little bit of washing, a superficial tidying of Madeline's room, being careful not to disturb the boxes of embroidery, the needles and thread that lay carefully arranged according to Madeline's mental filing system.

Miller dropped her at the kiosk and she walked slowly through the gardens. She could go to the beach and sunbathe or swim this afternoon, if she wanted.

She hoped Andrew wouldn't call, because she felt strangely vulnerable and alone, now that Dain Lammont wasn't in his cabin and Madeline was gone.

She heard the sound of chattering and laughter as she

gathered her small armful of washing. It came in small bursts as people passed, and it sounded far away, like the language of another world.

Despite Victor's reassurance, her heart ached for Madeline, and the moment of truth that must be faced if that medical report wasn't all she hoped for.

'I care,' Karen admitted to herself fiercely, 'I care as if she were my own mother,' and she saw the cabin walls through a mist of tears.

Then she went into her own room, picked up night-dress and briefs to fling on top of her armful of washing; and when she walked to the cabin door, Andrew stood there, face flushed, a wide smile of triumph curving his lips, a newspaper in his hand.

He said, 'Get a load of this, Karo,' and pushed his way inside, knocking some of the clothes out of her hand. He breathed fast and deep, as if he had run far.

Karen protested, 'Hey, watch it, please!' but he ignored her. He flipped the newspaper on to the table, jabbing a page with one finger, and then he said, 'There's your mate, Dain Lammont, I'll bet a thousand dollars.'

'What is?'

'This fellow, the one they've written about. This is today's news, from the mainland. I waited to get a paper at the resort.' His voice thickened with ill-concealed triumph. 'He's a bail-jumper, that's what he is. A thief. Swindled people out of millions in some kind of fake property development on the Reef. Seems it's his favourite playground. He's in for years in jail, if they catch him, and they will.'

Karen sat down weakly. She said in a small voice, 'Don't be ridiculous.'

'I'm not being ridiculous. Get a load of this.' He grabbed the paper, crumpling it in his hand, and his eyes were vindictive. He read:

'Man wanted for questioning . . . there's a description here, it fits Dain Lammont . . . Fraud Squad detectives have issued a warrant alleging theft . . . also want to interview the man about land ventures and motel deals . . . Bail of $150,000 . . . police are seeking the fugitive somewhere on the Barrier Reef . . . The wanted man has been known to use several aliases . . .' He pushed the paper spitefully towards her. 'Like I said, they'll get him.'

Karen left the newspaper lying crumpled on the table. 'How do you know?'

Now Andrew was triumphant. 'Because I phoned the mainland straight away, as soon as I read it. I told them where to look.' He waved a hand in the direction of Dain's cabin. 'All they have to do is post a twenty-four-hour watch on that place and bingo! they'll grab their man.'

He watched her face, searching it avidly for reaction.

Karen said, 'You don't know he's their man. Is there a photograph?'

'No, but there's a clear description, and it fits. Here, read it for yourself if you won't listen to me.'

'Does it say his name?'

'Not the one he's using here, but it mentions that he uses false names. David something, it says, is his real name. But it's him, all right. Want to bet?'

She didn't want to read it. She felt sick, limbs, body and heart suddenly ice-cold. Zero, she thought. Nothing. Absolute nothing. You can't trust anybody. But hadn't she known all along that she couldn't trust Dain Lammont?

Andrew quoted figures—hundreds of thousands of dollars, into millions. 'He's been mighty clever.' Was there a touch of envy in his voice? 'The man must be a flipping genius!'

A rat, but a clever rat. That was what he suggested . . .

Karen picked up the newspaper and thrust it towards Andrew.

'Go away, please.'

'What?'

'Go away. Oh, please, do go away. Can't you see I'm busy?'

She bent to collect the dropped pieces of washing. It didn't look as if it would keep her very busy, Andrew's look said. She gestured with her head towards the door.

'Go now,' she demanded, and because of something in her voice, he pushed his chair away angrily and stood up. But he didn't collect his newspaper. He left it there to taunt her. And in the doorway he paused, self-righteous and angry, before he fired his parting shot.

'You just don't want to know,' he accused bitterly, and turned on his heel.

Like an automaton Karen walked to the laundry, put her coins in the washing machine, waited for it to produce her clean washing, and hung it out to dry. Her body was numb, but her mind was racing.

If Andrew was right, there would be men waiting for Dain when next he came to Great Keppel. Trained men, waiting to spring the trap Andrew had helped set. And why not—didn't he deserve it?

A man who could with coolness and calculation fleece untold wealth from trusting investors. A shrewd operator. Yes, Dain would be all of those. She had seen it in his eyes, his hard mouth, his overbearing manner.

'A Heathcliff of a man,' Madeline had called him. But Karen had seen laughter lurking in Dain Lammont's eyes—laughter and fleeting gentleness in his manner towards the young deaf boy who was probably his son.

By the time her washing flapped on the line, Karen knew what she was going to do. She didn't ask herself whether it was right or wrong, she simply recognised that it was imperative.

She walked to the beach and found Miller outside his boatshed, arranging jet-skis for public hire. She said, 'Miller, the boat——' and he pulled a surprised face, and said 'What, again!' but he turned to walk with her to the shed where the motor was stored and the oars. 'I don't want it now. In about an hour, say, or a little more.'

Karen had remembered the few small jobs she had promised herself to do in the cabin; and Miller looked at the sky and the way the scattered clouds were moving, and said, 'There'll be a blow later. Can't it want until tomorrow?'

'No, really, Miller, it's terribly important. There isn't going to be a—a storm or anything, is there?'

He squinted at the horizon where fingers of white cloud poked into the blue and said, 'No, no storms. Just a little temporary turbulence, that's all. Nothing you can't handle, if you don't mind a bit of splash.'

His grin was wide and generous and understanding.

'Something vital come up, has it, sweetheart?'

She said yes and knew he thought it a joke. Miller liked to tease, but he was solid and reliable as a rock, and that was a change from some other people she knew.

She said, 'An hour, then,' and he nodded.

'She'll be ready.'

There was a girl with a strong bronze body and waist-length sun-bleached hair sitting on the beach waiting for Miller, and he winked at Karen and blew a kiss towards the girl; and Karen's mouth made an 'O'

of surprise, because Miller didn't usually spend much
time looking at girls.

He'd told her once that his guitar was his lady, but
now he set about refilling the fuel tank and when it
was done he walked jauntily over to the girl with long
blonde hair; and Karen mused, 'Somebody's happy.'

She was pleased for Miller. Even if it proved only a
passing romance, as it well might, she thought it was
some kind of compensation that while her own hopes
had tumbled down, Miller who was staunch and kind
should have found himself a little dream to colour his
time.

Back in the cabin, she whisked through her chores,
then pulled on the rose denim jeans and pink windcheater over her yellow T-shirt, because Miller had
suggested rising wind, and that meant coolness when
she got out of the island's shelter.

The sky was covered now in speckled clouds, like
little puffs of white smoke, and Miller, who was still
chatting up the handsome blonde, came rushing to help
her drag the boat into the water.

He said, 'Sure it can't wait? This will blow over
soon,' and Karen said no, she didn't think it could
wait, but she would be careful.

'You couldn't even give it half an hour?'

She shook her head, laughing, and he saluted as the
motor spluttered into life and she took off in a shower
of white spray.

She wasn't sure how she managed the laugh that
satisfied Miller, because she wasn't certain herself that
what she was doing was sensible and sane. Dain might
laugh her off his island when she came to him with
that silly story. But if it were true, and he did happen
to be the fugitive the police were searching for, then
she ought to warn him. Quickly. For Leon's sake.

Although the wind was fresher than usual, the channel bouncier, Karen enjoyed her trip out to Blunteree. She didn't go there directly, of course. She veered between other islands, making a wide sweep in one direction, and then back again, because there were other craft on the ocean, and she didn't want to lead anybody to Dain's secret island.

It was only as she approached Blunteree that her heart missed a beat. The reef was covered with what Miller called 'chop'—a wild swirling of shallow water.

Karen reduced speed, travelling as slowly as she dared across the churning water, crouching to protect herself from flying spray. But to her surprise the small boat bobbed over the turbulence without too much trouble.

Once or twice she felt the dinghy swing under her, as some erratic current forced it to yaw, but she held course with reasonable control, although her wrists ached when she finally slid on to calmer water inside the reef.

She stretched the fingers of one hand, releasing tension, then the other, expelling breath in a long sigh of relief. She must have been very tense back there with the aluminium boat hitting the waves in a series of sharp bounces that reverberated through her body, making her spine tingle. Now it was over, the final part of the journey easy going.

When the bow of the boat scraped on the pebbles, she jumped out quickly and pulled it above the tideline.

Her jeans were wet to the knees, and she rolled them before going to the back of the cove to take a look at the climb to the top of the island.

The pandanus palms rattled spiky leaves. They bore fruit like miniature pineapples on the end of each stiff branch, and their buttress roots made triangles of thick tubes at the base of each tree, so that they looked like multi-legged men, stiff and tall, guarding Dain Lammont on his island.

Karen shook off the fancy and began to climb. If she thought too much, if she studied the doubt in her mind, she might turn and run, because she could be making a prize idiot of herself, and Dain would be the first to let her know if that happened.

She gritted her teeth and climbed; and when she reached the top she looked around, seeking direction. She should be able to find Dain's hut. Blunteree was, after all, a very small island.

She hurried through the casuarinas without even noticing their wailing in the wind, then down into the hollow with its denser bushland. The gumtrees made a great noise, shaking their branches so that the scent of eucalyptus floated everywhere.

Last time, she had noticed the shadows in late afternoon had all pointed towards the pebbled beach. Today was different—cloudy sky, diffused shadows. Very confusing, once she lost sight of the rim of the island. That would be a great stroke, wouldn't it, to get lost on her errand of mercy.

But her feet seemed to find the right direction of their own accord, and soon she encountered one familiar tree, then another, as if she had an inbuilt compass behind her eyes, or perhaps her intentions guided her. And when the breeze disturbed the thick foliage of a leaning tree, revealing the side of Dain's wooden hut, it didn't really surprise her.

She had expected it to happen that way.

CHAPTER EIGHT

WHAT Karen hadn't expected was the thunder on Dain's face after she thumped on the door of his hut, pushed open the unlocked door with its dangling padlock and chain, and finding no one inside walked over to the dividing door and banged on it so desperately the hut echoed with the sound.

He flung open the door and glowered at her, and behind him she saw a desk, a typewriter, stacks of papers in what looked like wild disorder.

She backed away as Leon came skipping in to the hut, and because Dain turned his scowling face towards Leon, Karen put herself between them; but Dain was coming no farther. He halted in the doorway, and there were smudges around his eyes as if he had been concentrating too long. There was darkness on his lean face; and he hadn't shaved. His lips were tight and pale.

He blinked at her, then turned to glance behind him, as if he was worried what she might have seen.

'Whatever you're doing in there,' she challenged him, 'you'd better lock the door on it, and come out here and pay some attention.'

His eyes flicked over her, boring into her, before he turned and closed the door and came slowly into the main part of the hut.

Leon watched every movement. He had flung himself towards Karen, laughing, but it had not needed Dain's lowering expression to wipe away the laughter. There was an atmosphere in the hut, a feeling of tension. Karen supposed she had brought it with her.

She tried a comforting smile at the boy and he nodded and offered a faint grin, but he was watchful.

Dain walked to the rough wooden table, lit a cigarette, inhaled, exhaled, all the time studying her.

'Now,' he ordered, 'let's hear it, whatever it is. And it had better be good.'

Karen glanced doubtfully at Leon, and Dain raised an eyebrow and gestured at the billycan where it sat beside the stove, and the boy picked it up obediently and went outside to fill it from the water tank.

Once Karen was satisfied Leon could not read her lips to know what she was saying, she told Dain, 'There are two men looking for you at Wapparaburra. One of them has a camera.'

'Did you talk to them?'

'No. They asked Jenna, yesterday——' she swallowed nervously. 'They—they described a person they were looking for, and it sounded like you.'

'So? It probably was me. But if you didn't tell them anything, and neither did Jenna, why the big deal?'

He wasn't sneering. If he'd become any more hostile, or accused her of wasting his time, Karen knew she would have retreated at once. Now she was here, it didn't seem in any way credible that the man facing her could be a swindler, a cheat, a man on the run from justice.

Then she recalled his mysterious behaviour, his strange reticence, and she blurted reluctantly, 'There's more. I suppose I'd better tell you. Andrew bought a newspaper at the resort today and—and there were headlines about a man running away from the police. Some sort of—some sort of confidence man, I think, who's been into bogus land development and got off with a lot of people's money. And he said—Andrew, that is—he thinks it's you, and he's rung the police at

Rockhampton and Yeppoon. Because they think he—
this man—is hiding out somewhere along the Reef.'

'Oh.' He studied her intently, giving nothing away.
'And have you told Andrew or anyone else about your
little jaunt out here?'

'No, of course I haven't!'

'Splendid. That's one thing you've done right.' Dain
didn't seem very alarmed. Instead, he became unexpectedly solicitous about her welfare. She must have
looked distraught, because he looked keenly into her
face and said, 'Sit down,' and when she hesitated he
changed instantly back into the man she knew, and
snarled, 'Sit down, for God's sake! You're exhausted.'

He pushed a bench back from the table and Karen
sat down weakly, but his snappish order had stirred
resentment, and she faced him defiantly.

He moved towards the closed door, studying her
through half-closed eyes, and she thought, 'I was right.
You're a cool person.'

Finally he asked, 'Does Madeline know you're
here?'

'No. She went to Rockhampton with Victor. You
knew she was going, don't you remember? For the
check-up. She's staying overnight on the mainland.'

Dain raised his eyebrows. 'Leaving you alone?'

She said scornfully, 'I'm a grown woman,' and his
mouth twitched.

Then he said, 'Leon will come back any minute, and
we'll have a cup of tea, because you look as if you
could do with one. Meanwhile, you understand I can't
let you go back to Great Keppel after what you've told
me. You might tell someone else. It's too much of a
risk.'

Karen stared at him aghast.

'Don't be utterly stupid! If you are that man—that
swindler, whatever he is—you'd be pretty silly to add

kidnapping to your crimes. Haven't you committed enough already?'

If you are that man, she'd been careful to say. So she wasn't accusing him. Not exactly. Perhaps he would imagine she wasn't certain of her facts; she certainly hoped so, and she had better go on being light-hearted about it, because he stood there, watchful and grim, and she was having uneasy feelings about him again.

She mumbled, 'I don't care who you are, or what you've done either. I simply thought—well, I thought, what would happen to Leon if the police arrest you. Mistakenly, of course,' she added hurriedly, and he smiled, a grim smile without any humour.

'I see.' His voice became more ironic. 'It was extremely kind of you to be so concerned about Leon. Now we'd better decide what else we can do to further ensure Leon's safety, I think. Don't you?'

Karen didn't like the way he was surveying her. Her knees became unaccountably weak.

He said, 'You came in Miller's boat, of course?' and she nodded meekly.

'It will have to be taken back to Wapparaburra, to his boatshed. But that's no problem. I have my dinghy here. The wind is wearing itself out; it should drop any minute now. So I'll tow Miller's boat back where he'll find it safe and sound, and you can stay overnight with us on Blunteree while I decide what to do after I deliver you back on Great Keppel tomorrow morning. About Madeline—she'll come back to Keppel on the midday plane tomorrow, I take it.'

'Yes, but——'

'That should give me time to work something out. I mean, if I can pull a huge swindle like you're talking about, I should be able to hoodwink a couple of dumb policemen.'

Karen contradicted frostily, 'Policemen aren't dumb,' and he grimaced.

'True, but irrelevant. I only meant, I intended to make them look dumb. I hope.'

Karen's heart sank. He must be the man they were looking for—surely he was telling her so? Talking down about policemen. Making plans to escape. But he was cool, not flustered in any way.

On the contrary, he had become clear-thinking, powerful, as if he were one of those people who react dynamically to danger, pulling himself together, becoming alert and alive under pressure.

He was saying crisply, 'That's it, then. I'll tow Miller's boat and gear back to his shed and he'll know you're safe. We can't have him sending out a search party. There's a comfortable bunk here you can sleep on, I'll even offer you a sleeping-bag. I apologise for the inconvenience, but I'm afraid you're going to be my prisoner for the night.'

'Very melodramatic,' Karen sniffed. 'If you're dashing off with Miller's boat, how do you know I'll be here when you get back?'

'Because I trust you to look after Leon.' His face was stern. 'I suppose I should ask you, is there anything you want brought back from Great Keppel?'

'No, thank you.' Her eyes smouldered. Dain hesitated, then, rubbing his lower lip with a sunbrowned finger as though the coldly inflexible Dain Lammont might—miracle of miracles—have been a little unsure of himself.

He was dressed in faded denim jeans and an emerald T-shirt that said 'Wapparaburra for fun in the sun'; his hair was rumpled, as if he had been doing some heavy concentrating in that locked-up room, and those long browned fingers might have been running through the dark hair while he struggled to get his thoughts together. There were tired lines around eyes and mouth corners.

Whatever he had been doing, it seemed a fair sort of guess that things weren't working out easily.

He caught her looking at him and his eyes gleamed.

'Tell me honestly, is there any special reason why you shouldn't stay here on Blunteree with us until tomorrow?'

'There's no reason why I shouldn't go back to Great Keppel now.'

'That's not what I asked you.'

Still he hovered, as he asked, 'Does the prospect of staying here fill you with terror?'

She met his eyes disdainfully, her expression haughty. 'Nothing you could do would fill me with terror.'

'That's a debatable point.'

She didn't miss the sardonic undertone in his voice. And when she remembered her last visit and the way it had ended . . . how he had held her and kissed her, and the feeling it had generated, she stared at him doubtfully, with a lot of her confidence evaporating.

'You'll be safe here.'

He meant she wouldn't be swallowed up by a tidal wave or carried away in a cyclone. Was that what he really meant? Karen inspected him cautiously, questing amber eyes searching his features for some inkling of his meaning. Could he be speaking personally, assuring her, You will be quite safe from me?

She bit her lip. He seemed to take pleasure in making her feel uncomfortable.

When Leon came back with his billy, and the water boiled, Dain made mugs of tea, and Leon pantomimed the movements of some bird he had seen outside. Or was it a butterfly? He made his hands into wings, fluttered, signing his meaning to Dain.

Then Dain said conversationally, 'We have a pair of oyster birds who visit us. Leon is trying to tame them, but he isn't having much luck.'

He swallowed his mug of hot tea quickly, gave Leon more sign instructions, then said, 'I should be back in less than an hour. You might try to have a meal cooked by then.'

'I might not.'

'In that case,' he answered reasonably, 'you'll go to bed hungry.'

Watching him stride away into the heavy scrub, Karen was aware of an odd feeling of deprivation.

He should have stayed. It wouldn't have done any harm if Miller had taken another boat and come seeking her, because Miller hadn't any idea where she was; but she realised with a sinking heart that if his boat stayed missing he might become alarmed for her safety and start a full-scale search.

So Dain had been wise to tow Miller's dinghy back to Great Keppel. Miller, finding it there, would deduce she had arrived safely home. Clever thinking, Karen decided. Quick and clever thinking by a shrewd and devious man.

Instinct told her that if she'd performed—put on a really good act to show she was distressed by the prospect of spending the night on Blunteree—then Dain would have quietly taken her back.

So she had made some kind of choice when she calmly allowed him to carry out his plan of towing Miller's boat back. Just as she had made a choice when she elected to set out for Blunteree with her warning as soon as Andrew had flounced away.

She walked back into the driftwood hut. Leon was occupied washing out mugs. He waved a hand towards the stove, making gestures to signify eating and drinking, his young mouth curved in teasing pleasure. He was delighted to have her here, his dancing eyes told her.

Storage arrangements were primitive but neat. A small kerosene refrigerator held plastic boxes of fish. There was milk, fruit and vegetables and a carton of coleslaw, but the only meat was hard-frozen. So Dain must mean her to cook some of the fish.

Karen selected a panful of thick white fillets; she peeled potatoes, sliced tomatoes and onions, Leon hovering near, gathering up peels and scraps, taking them outside to offer to his birds.

Dain had still not arrived when the cooking was done, and at Leon's silent coaxing Karen covered the pans, leaving everything to keep warm.

Leon led her to the beach along the track which he read perfectly, never hesitating when the trees loomed around them and light dimmed.

It was sunset when Dain came back across the reef. His dinghy, like Miller's, skated easily over the shallow water. As Dain predicted the wind had dropped, the sea lay mirror-calm except for the plume of white wash that spread out behind the boat.

There were splashes of orange where the sun floated on the horizon, and smudges of purple cloud with edges glittering gold behind the distant shape that was Great Keppel Island.

The wash from Dain's dinghy as he turned in to shore rattled the white pebbles, then a ripple slid in and touched the feet of the pandanus palms before it rustled back into the sea. The rock pools were filmed with gold.

Seeing Dain arrive, Leon scrambled recklessly down to help the tall man secure his boat. As Dain moved, his lean body became a silhouette, like a black cut-out, against the light. Karen watched fascinated as the two figures below, the long and the short, moved swiftly to stow away dinghy and motor.

No wonder she hadn't seen it when she landed; it was cunningly concealed behind a group of stunted trees that hid it completely.

The man and the boy climbed the cliffs to where Karen waited. Dain climbed easily, carrying the oars, disdaining to grasp at stunted trees as Karen had been forced to do.

He asked, 'Where's my dinner? Don't tell me you've decided I can starve,' and she answered stiffly, 'It's on the stove, keeping warm, and that's more than you deserve.'

They had almost reached the hut when she ventured the question she so much wanted to ask.

'Did you see Miller? Did you tell him I'm all right? I suppose you thought up some devious explanation.'

For a few seconds she thought he wasn't going to answer, then he shook his head, his eyes cynical.

'Didn't go near the kiosk, Golden Hair. Not a policeman in sight, nor Miller either. But I delivered the boat. Everything is back in its proper place.' They were walking in through the doorway when he added softly, 'Except you, of course. Unless you feel this is your rightful place.'

When she didn't answer he said briskly, 'Where's that meal you promised? I could eat an elephant.'

'You won't get an elephant. They're pretty scarce around here. You won't even get steak. I hope you appreciate fish, because that's all I could find.'

'What's the matter, Golden Hair? Don't you like fish?'

'Of course I do, especially fresh from the sea. It's just that—I've eaten so much fish in the last few days it's a wonder I haven't grown fins.'

He grinned at that, a bleak sort of amusement with the eyes still remote.

'That seems appropriate for a mermaid.'

He was reaching down dishes, arranging them on the table, and Karen pulled a face at him.

'Tin plates?' she scoffed. 'Not very grand.'

'I thought they seemed quite suitable. After all, you're not exactly dressed for dinner.'

Critically he surveyed the jeans with their rolled-up cuffs, the salt-splashed windcheater.

'Tell you what, Golden Hair. When all this is over, if I escape the long arm of the law, I promise faithfully to treat you to a good steak dinner. Sign of my gratitude.'

'I can't wait.'

'Afraid you'll just have to,' he pointed out equably, sliding over the sarcasm in her voice as if it had never existed.

Dusk deepened halfway through the meal and they finished it by the light from a portable gas-lamp. Afterwards they went walking over the darkened island, because Dain decided Leon needed exercise, and when they returned he sent Leon to bed, hoisting him into the upper bunk.

He waited until Leon settled down, then went into his private room and came out with two sleeping-bags, one of which he tossed to Karen. He tucked the other under his arm and directed, 'The lower bunk is yours, and there's a pair of Leon's pyjamas folded inside the bag. I managed to sneak into our cabin at Keppel and get them for you. They're more your size than mine would be. If the sleeping-bag is too warm, use it as a mattress and pull the sheet over you, but I warn you the nights can get nippy out here.'

She asked sweetly, 'Have I stolen your bunk?' and he actually grinned.

'Don't apologise.'

'I wasn't going to,' she snapped, trying not to wonder where he was going to sleep. From the glimpse she'd had of his private room, there didn't seem any spare space in there. That left outside under the stars, or on the floor. The hard, hard floor. Her lips curved in a smile of pure pleasure.

'You're going to be uncomfortable,' she purred; and his answering laugh was derisive.

'Don't count on it, lady. I've slept on moving camels, mullock heaps, armoured tanks and in mosquito-ridden swamps. Sorry to disappoint you, but I shan't be at all uncomfortable.'

When she stood waiting for him to leave before she changed into the pyjamas he had given her, he shrugged and walked away saying, 'I'll be back in ten minutes to turn out the lamp. Not frightened in the dark, are you?'

She heard the rasp of the door, and took it that Dain had left, but just in case he hadn't she moved out from the spill of light flung by the lamp before stripping off her clothes.

Leon's pyjamas fitted reasonably well except for the legs, which left her legs bare well above the ankles. She was fastening the last button on the pyjama top when Dain pushed open the door and she felt rather than saw him walking into the lamplight.

She gasped, 'I'm not ready!' and he came out of the shadows, smiling faintly, saying, 'I can see that.'

Not to save her life could Karen have backed away as Dain came towards her. He was naked above the waist, the brown of his body blending into the darkness, lamplight casting planes of black and gold over his sharply-boned face, so that it became elusive, mysterious.

The clear sloping brows lent an exotic look as lamplight illusion extended them almost to the wavy hairline, accentuating the hard jaw, the hollowed eyes. The powerful body seemed to have something alien about it, as if a stranger had walked into the hut from the darkness outside.

Yet his smile when it came was a generous flash of gleaming white that lit his whole face with amusement.

'Not quite your size, but very alluring.' He was looking at the pyjamas, and Karen wanted to dive into the bunk and cover herself with the sleeping-bag; but even through the unexpected softness of his smiling he was forbidding it.

He stood quietly assessing her, willing her to stand there, and once he probed his lower lip with his tongue, as if he might have been about to say something. Then he reached out a hand and smoothed her hair.

Karen darted a glance at Leon's bunk, but the boy was fast asleep.

It was so quiet in the cabin that she heard Dain's breathing and her own. It hit her like a shock from sudden thunder that if she screamed Leon wouldn't hear her. No matter how desperately she might need help, she would have to touch Leon, shake him into consciousness, before he could be aware of her need.

With a gasp of distress, she pulled away from the touch of Dain's hand, but he stayed her by twining his fingers deeper in her hair. He leaned down and she heard one frightened leap of her own heart as he kissed her gently on the forehead.

Then he put her away from him and her pulse steadied while fear died away.

'I told you you'd be safe,' he whispered. 'Now hop into the bunk like a good little girl while I turn out the lamp.'

He walked into his own room while Karen arranged herself in the sleeping-bag on the bunk, then Dain came back carrying a torch.

'In case you want to walk about in the night,' he

explained softly. 'And don't forget I might be sleeping on the floor if the mosquitoes get hungry outside, so please don't tumble over me.'

He turned out the lamp and she heard his footsteps recede across the floor. The door rasped again. The bunk was narrow but comfortable, and because Karen had not expected to sleep she woke up some time in the middle of the night with a start of wild surprise.

Dain moved quietly on the other side of the hut, spreading out his sleeping-bag in the centre of a broad beam of moonlight, and suddenly she wanted to giggle.

She almost called, 'Were the mosquitoes hungry?' but afterwards she was glad she hadn't let the impulse carry her away, because the moonbeam widened, and she saw Dain naked.

Once, Leon rolled over in his bunk, and she thought Dain flung a quick glance their way, then Leon moved again, his bunk creaked faintly, and after that there was only silence.

Karen was first to wake in the morning. She wrapped the sleeping-bag around her and went to the shower outside, which was cold; but when she came back into the hut the other two were awake and dressed, Leon still rubbing sleep from his eyes, but Dain looking as if he had slept long and well. He still needed a shave, and he had filled the billy to heat water, and he looked at Karen jeeringly as she came in.

'Spartan, are you? Cold showers at daybreak,' but Karen ignored him. He should have warned her how icily cold the water was. She would have left her shower until she was back in the comforts of Wapparaburra, and she flung him a hostile glare before she went to the cupboard to see what she could find for breakfast.

Dain said, 'We'll leave early for Great Keppel.

There's a king tide rising later. Also I think we'll slip away before too many people are about. We don't want to look conspicuous.'

He didn't say why; but he had reminded Karen that he was a fugitive, and she looked at him curiously, debating again whether he was one of those people stimulated by danger.

He appeared remarkably poised, whatever he was feeling; and afterwards as they sat in his boat heading towards Great Keppel, it looked to Karen that there was nothing on his mind but enjoyment of the boat's movement, the wind streaming in his hair, the sounds around him.

He wore the familiar jeans with open denim jacket, muscled chest braced against the boat's pull as they crossed the channel, its waters already seething as though the ocean moved restlessly in readiness for the king tide's rising.

When they neared Great Keppel, the boat swung around, heading for an unfamiliar beach, and Karen shouted into the wind, 'Hey, that's not——'

'Wapparaburra?' He shook his head. 'No. I decided we'd fish among the mangroves for a while. Nice secluded area, good place to lie low.'

When they reached the mouth of a large creek and glided cautiously in, Karen said crossly, 'I don't have to lie low.'

'No, but you've helped devour our fish, so you'll have to help replace them. You don't want to leave us with an empty cupboard, do you?'

'That's all right with me.' Her voice was indignant. 'I don't know how to fish and I don't want to learn.'

Out of sight from the sea, by a curve in the creek, Dain cut the motor and dropped anchor. Leon held out his hand for a line, but Karen snapped, 'You'd better hold the boat steady, I'm leaving.'

They were not very far from the banks, where glossy green-gold mangroves clutched the mud with exposed roots. The creek-bed, wide and shallow, looked inviting.

Dain drawled, faintly amused, 'Got webbed feet, have you?' and Karen stared at him, uncomprehending.

He waved a hand at the sandbanks around them. 'You'd have quite a time staggering through that slush. It's almost quicksand in places, when the tide isn't full in; like now. The sandbanks just wait there, like wet sponges, ready to trap the feet of the unwary.'

He could have been exaggerating, it was hard to tell, but the only way to test him was to lower herself over the side of the boat, and the thought of floundering in spongy sandtraps while he laughed was rather deflating. She wouldn't have much left of her dignity.

Crossly, she refused the baited line he offered her, but when he and Leon began hauling in fish she wished she had not been so hasty.

Dain Lammont caught only the fish he needed. When the rising tide began to skither over nearer sandbanks and swirl among the mangroves, he started the motor and set out for the open sea again.

He was careful not to take his boat all the way to Wapparaburra. Instead he pulled in halfway along a beach some distance from the cabins, making signs for Leon to stay with it.

He indicated Karen, then himself, pointing towards Wapparaburra; and Leon nodded cheerfully, evidently understanding that Dain would take Karen back while he, Leon, stood guard over the boat.

He carried the fishbasket to the water's edge and sat happily cleaning fish, while Karen looked away because she wasn't sure she wanted to watch.

Ridiculous to be so squeamish, she was upbraiding

herself, when she found the tall man beside them, and
he was looking down at Leon with an expression so
tender that she caught her breath. For the first time
she glimpsed a gentle man, a tender caring man, beneath the bleak exterior.

He turned to her and raised those winged brows in
mockery, erasing the betraying gentleness from his
expression, but she wasn't fooled.

As they walked away she said, 'You're not that man
at all, are you; the one they're looking for?'

For a fleeting instant his face revealed that he had
been taken by surprise, and there was something else,
some deeper emotion, that flashed and disappeared.

He said levelly, 'How do you know I'm not?'

'I'm not sure. Woman's intuition, perhaps.' He
didn't sneer, as she half expected, and she accused him,
'You could have told me. You didn't have to carry out
this—this ridiculous charade.'

'And missed our little interlude, our picnic?' She
thought his mouth faintly malicious. The gleam of
white teeth in suntanned features seemed to flash with
some overtones of derision.

'It may have been a picnic for you,' she retorted
icily, 'but I can assure you it wasn't for me.'

'What was it, then?' His eyes challenged hers.

'It was—it was an ordeal.'

'Is that so?'

He was laughing at her and she stalked away, walking faster, spurred by anger.

He caught her on the sandy track across the dunes,
where creeping vines made patterns of lavender-
coloured pea-flowers under her feet, so that she
stepped carefully, trying not to crush the delicate
blooms. He swung her around to face him, his mouth
perilously close to hers as he leaned over her.

'Liar!' he whispered. 'Don't tell me you didn't enjoy

it,' and she stood there petrified, despising herself for her helplessness but powerless to run from him.

She hoped he wouldn't hear the crazy beating of her heart under the T-shirt. Her lips parted, influenced by the powerful force of his body in an experience that had nothing to do with logic or sensibility, but was somehow part of the essence of the fragrant morning. She was caught in a wash of feeling that rose out of the scented atmosphere, the sea sound drifting over the dunes, so many different perfumes and whisperings all combined in a wave of sensuality that coalesced in the body of this one man. She stood helpless while his hands reached out and gripped her slender shoulders to pull her closer, until he had only to lean down his head and his lips would close over hers like the coming together of metal and magnet, the inevitable blending of sunlight and ocean, need and response. So right. So natural.

His hands slid down her arms from shoulders to wrists in slow caressing movements, shaping her into yielding, until she almost drowned in vibrant awareness of his touch, his nearness. Then, just as slowly, just as carelessly, he let her go, putting her firmly away from him, as if she had been the one making advances, and not he.

Disbelieving, Karen stared wildly at him, before she stumbled away. But he caught her, and this time she found herself being rough-handled as he swung her around to face him again.

'Feeling rejected, are we?'

He drew in his breath in a faint groaning sound when he saw that her eyes were filling with tears.

'Lord, what a crazy thing is woman! You don't know what a lucky escape you've had, Miss Tiger Eyes.'

. . . Tiger Eyes. Not Golden Hair . . . Not Andrew's gentle English lily.

Then Dain said mildly, 'They'll be looking out for you at Wapparaburra. I told Jenna I'd deliver you back early this morning. She thinks you've been visiting friends with me.'

'You told Jenna!' Karen gazed at him, bewildered, 'But you said—you said you didn't meet anybody when you brought back Miller's boat.'

'I told you I didn't talk to Miller and I didn't go near the kiosk. Both of which were true. I bumped into Jenna when I went to my cabin for Leon's spare pyjamas.'

Karen gathered her shaky dignity. 'Very devious!'

'Yes, wasn't it?' His voice was cheerful, unrepentant, 'Now we'd better get you back to your cabin before Jenna sends out the dog squad.'

They were threading their way through the bushland when Karen, having restored her composure, dared to demand, 'I suppose you wouldn't care to tell me who you are, and why you go to the trouble of using false names. I mean, you're obviously up to something underhanded.'

This time his smile was faint.

'It's all very simple, really. Very simple, and no doubt a little bit silly.' He reached out for a paperbark branch, holding it back until she passed. 'I'm a fairly innocuous person—a television news reporter, working for a current affairs programme, member of a five-man team.' He grinned suddenly. 'Four men and one woman, actually,' he amended. 'Sally does the women's affairs, but she's a bright girl, is Sally, getting her teeth into a few meaty things as well, and good luck to her.'

'Unfortunately, she does a bit of P.R. work—public relations—and keeps sending people up for interviews, sometimes at the wrong moment. Like at present. I'm not long back from a stint in one of the more poverty-stricken countries, and I have something I want to say and show urgently while it's fresh in my mind. So when I feel like that I hide myself away. You know where.'

'Oh.' It sounded plausible. Karen pursed her lips and asked the next question cautiously.

'What about the false names? Just cover-up?'

'More or less.' He stayed silent for a few steps before he said quietly, 'I like my privacy, so occasionally I become John Brown or Smith. And I do a bit of scriptwriting on the side, under another name, Rockard Barrington. It won't mean anything to you, you being a—um—foreigner, but it's becoming quite well known in the Australian TV world. It's a wonder Jenna didn't pick it up. Anyway, there you are.'

He spread out his hands in a gesture of innocence. 'Now you know all. No criminal activities. Not that anybody's discovered yet, anyway.'

Karen thought about that, quietly, all the way over the sandhills to the Wapparaburra cabins.

Surprisingly, for she recognised him as a complicated, complex man, she didn't for a moment doubt his word. He carried the air of a man who had accomplished things, and had seen much. His sojourn in an underprivileged country had probably sent him home with that lean, hollow-faced look, and was no doubt responsible for the disillusion in his eyes.

He said very little for the remainder of the walk, presumably leaving her to think over what he had told her.

He hadn't mentioned why he considered it necessary to conduct last night's charade. Possibly a warped sense of humour, Karen decided crossly, but she walked ahead of him along the white track, her animosity slowly dispersing, so that she found no more questions to ask of him.

At Madeline's door he held out his hand.

'Got your key? I'll take a look inside and make sure there are no intruders hiding in your cupboards.'

She handed him the key. 'Where will you go now?'

'Back to Blunteree. I've work to do, remember?'

That made her feel guilty. He was talking about the work he might have completed had she not dashed off in her impetuous haste to interrupt him on his island.

'I'm sorry.'

Dain turned the key, slid back the glass door.

'Why?'

'I could have saved your time, and mine, instead of chasing after you. It was all for nothing, wasn't it?'

'I wouldn't say that.' He was mocking again, eyes ironic, reminding her . . .

Karen offered hastily, 'Would you care for a drink—lemonade, tea or coffee?'

'Thank you, no. Leon is waiting for me.' He strode inside the cabin, checked the rooms, came outside. 'Goodbye for now. Promise you won't tell anyone where I've gone?'

He was goading her, like a mischievous schoolboy. She frowned at him.

'Not if they beg me.' And she flounced inside the cabin, sliding the door shut in his face.

She felt him stride away, across the gardens to his own cabin. Felt him, not saw him, reacting to his movements as if she had a bleeper under her skin that was attuned to him, and him only, so that she had this extraordinary picture of him striding away, turning on to the white path, arriving outside his cabin, raising an arm to shield his tall body from hanging fern baskets. She visualised it so clearly that it made her angry; and she gathered towel and toiletries and concentrated on freshening up before she prepared for Madeline, taking her time about it, as if she might have been trying to wash away disturbing recollections.

It was only as she begun setting the table for lunch that Karen recalled Dain's odd remark about inspecting the cabin. In case you have intruders in your cupboards, he had said . . .

Had he been thinking about Andrew, wanting to know whether Andrew waited for her? She decided he hadn't. Only a jealous man would have those kind of thoughts, and Dain had no reason to be jealous or overprotective about her.

Perversely, however, the idea lifted her spirits.

She went over the memory of those disturbing encounters when he had aroused her so very quickly, beyond anything she had ever known. He must have been aware of what he was doing, he was a very perceptive man.

She had been far too much under his spell—momentarily, of course, she reminded herself—to hide her responses from him. Oh yes, he had known. He could have captured her then.

Even the recall did strange things to her composure. A smile curved her lips as she readied the cabin for Madeline's return, dreaminess coming down on her like an unexpected glow.

She tried to be sensible about it, telling herself not to read too much into the casual kissing of a man much travelled, very experienced in the way of the world and probably in the ways of women also. She sighed. She should have learned by now not to build dreams on shaky foundations.

But surely that didn't mean you couldn't believe in happiness at all. The Dain Lammont who had stroked her into that mind-boggling awareness this morning was a far different man from the reticent stranger who had disappeared so frostily into his cabin the first night they met.

Surely that must mean something . . . that there was hope . . .

All the same, he had signed no contract, made no promises. On the contrary, he had assured her she had had a lucky escape. Only she hadn't escaped at all. She knew that now.

She stood quietly in the cabin, listening to Madeline's clock ticking on the bedside table, and honesty told her what she had felt for Andrew had been a mild experience compared with the way Dain had excited her senses this morning.

Her love for Andrew had been a young girl's love, a young girl's dreaming . . .

What she now felt for Dain was reality, and much more complex; a total engagement of mind and emotions and sensuality.

Dain had spun a web around her senses, sharpening perceptions, so that everywhere she found new vibrance, a new dimension to familiar things. There was so much she wanted to share with him, to please him, to be pleased by him.

This was powerful loving; and she was afraid of it, knowing now that love sometimes led to a closed door and unfulfilled promises. Yet she was quite sure that had Dain come loping down the path, holding out his arms to her, she would have gone to him and let the loving flow from her to him, so that he would know exactly how she felt.

She stood quite still, trembling. Outside the cabin door, a small brown bird sought nectar in a scarlet flower, probing so deeply that he almost disappeared among the trumpet petals.

Karen hoped Dain was watching. She wanted him to see everything, every beautiful thing the valley provided, so that he would be excited, too.

She whispered his name and then, 'I love you', and after that, 'Oh lord, what am I thinking about?' because it seemed impossible that she could be lifted from despair to this bright joy.

She thought of how Dain had touched her, and her cheeks burned at her own wanton thoughts. Then she steadied herself ... deliberately ... making a gigantic effort to push the turmoil from her emotions.

'Take it quietly,' she advised herself. But she could hope a little. Just a little. Dain had certainly made no commitment, but he had told her things he hadn't disclosed to anyone else, she was sure.

Her heart said, So he could care, couldn't he? and then the voice of reason, cool and calm, reminded her, 'Of course he may not have told you everything.'

CHAPTER NINE

THE clock jolted Karen back to practical things. Time to prepare lunch, it reminded her. Then off to the airstrip, because if Madeline's news wasn't good, she might need some moral support.

There were fillet steaks and fruit yoghurt and fresh bananas, and when everything was ready but the steaks she changed into white shorts and an embroidered cheesecloth blouse, and tied her hair into two ponytails, one on either side of her face, with white ribbons.

Miller whistled appreciatively when he saw her. 'Very cheeky,' he said. He had stopped the four-wheel-drive outside the kiosk, and he offered, 'Hop in, sweetheart. Can't promise you a lift back. I think we'll be full up.'

They arrived just as the bush pilot's plane banked

above the beach and glided down to earth. Afterwards, Karen was to remember that plane flashing gold in the sunlight as it descended, and wonder why she felt no premonition, no cold clear pain warning her of approaching disaster.

As it was, she watched the passengers alight, feeling a little anxious about Madeline, certainly paying only scant attention to the girl who walked towards Miller's four-wheel-drive as if it were her own personal chauffeur-driven Rolls-Royce.

She was taller than Karen, possibly more than a few years older, and she wore a skintight turquoise blue sheath with side-split skirt and a daring neckline that featured only one narrow strap across her left shoulder, leaving the other bare. Her hair was an artfully tumbled mass of short blonde curls held in place with an encircling gold and turquoise band, low on her forehead. Slender shoes with stiletto heels completed the stunning outfit.

She was slender and eye-catching and beamed out chic and confidence, and Miller rolled his eyes at Karen in exaggerated reaction; but Karen waited for Madeline and she let the other girl pass without paying her much attention at all; and that, of course, was a mistake.

Victor alighted before Madeline, and Karen tried to read his face. He smiled gently, that was all. He wasn't really telling her anything.

Madeline was last to alight, and when she stepped into the reception area beside Karen she said,

'Ask me.'

'So what did the doctor say? Tell me, please.'

Miller came back to listen, and when Madeline said, 'Good news—all clear!' he cheered and pumped her hand enthusiastically, and then he sobered. 'Does that mean we're going to lose you?'

'Not quite yet. I'm to have another week's rest, then look out, world, here I come!'

They hugged each other, Madeline and Karen, eyes bright with unshed tears, because this was an important moment for both of them.

Then Madeline said, 'Where's my escort?' and Victor and Miller took an arm each and took her triumphantly to the jeep. Madeline wore one of her casual floating dresses, a light silk in pale green splashed with apricot, and as she arranged herself beside Miller in the front seat, her face turned to Karen, smooth and smiling, all tension erased.

Miller had a full load of passengers and luggage. The girl in turquoise sat in the back, seemingly indifferent to all the fussing around her and to her fellow passengers.

Miller offered Karen an apologetic lift of his shoulders. 'No room for you, darling. Full load for the cabins today; but the walk will do you good.' He gave her an impudent grin. 'Exercise those lovely legs, it will.'

He drove past the resort onto the beach, while Karen took the path to Wapparaburra. She strolled slowly, thoughtfully.

Madeline would soon be well, and she rejoiced for her, but her own future had become insecure. In another week or so, she would have to look for another job or admit defeat and return home to England.

Her mother would be sympathetic at first, then angry with Andrew, and Karen knew she didn't want to go home. Not for a long, long time. She wanted to stay here, in Wapparaburra, on the island with its bushland and beautiful gardens, the white beaches and Miller's boat.

She wouldn't search deeply into her feelings for

other reasons. That was enough, that her heart ached at the thought of leaving.

By the time she arrived at the cabin, she had hidden her anxieties behind a happy face. This was Madeline's day. She poured cold drinks and put the steaks on to sizzle, and then she demanded, 'Now tell me, I want to hear everything that happened.'

'Wonderful news. The best I could get.' Madeline put her glass on the table and stretched out her arms, with their wide kimono sleeves gracefully falling; and she announced, 'You are looking at a walking miracle. According to my doctor, who should know. He gave me a thorough overhaul, and I'm hale and healthy in every way—blood pressure down, heart behaving splendidly.'

She chuckled. 'He's put me on a diet, because I'm larger than most women my age, but you might as well try to shrink the Taj Mahal. I was born to be plump. However, I promised to make an effort. No more cream cakes, no sugary desserts and not too much bread. That's as far as I will go.'

Her voice sang with relief and happiness. 'He's taken me off tablets, I shouldn't need them any more. Now I can plan that trip to England we talked about. Can you imagine, no more needlework! I'll become the world's most inquisitive tourist instead.'

Karen laughed. 'You mean my fantastic sketches will all finish up in the wastepaper basket?'

'Not at all. I'm quite interested in those canvas pictures, and I'll probably come back to them for relaxation, but I can't promise to do anything about that repulsive snake of yours.'

'I must admit, he isn't nearly as handsome as Francis Taupongi's creations.'

'You know how I feel, my dear, I'm sure. I don't have those reins tugging at me, holding me back, ordering Have patience. For a little while I'll allow myself the luxury of pretending I'll never have to look another needle in the eye. Oh dear, that's a pun.'

'Deplorable, but it should be excused today.'

Madeline spread her hands on the table, her laughter a little shamefaced. 'We are excited, aren't we?'

'Of course we are, and so we should be. It's wonderful news, and now we'll celebrate with lunch. Do you want to rest this afternoon?'

'I want to sit outside, with idle hands, and watch the passing parade. We have some new people in the camp, haven't we?'

Still with no premonition of disaster, Karen answered, 'Yes, several new arrivals.' How was she to guess that one of them would bring her grief?

Even when they sat outside after lunch, waiting for Victor who had gone to call on his friends, even then the day seemed calm and innocent, the peace unshatterable.

Madeline sat with a book beside her, not bothering to turn the pages, and Karen offered laughingly, 'If you want me to read, I'm available.' Madeline said No; and then they hard the tapping of stiletto heels on the cement path and a clear cold voice called, 'I say, where is Mr Lammont?'

It was the girl from the plane, the eye-catching blonde. She swept towards them, crossing the clipped grass instead of following the path all the way, so that she carelessly broke off a pink hibiscus as she passed and Karen felt her ego prickle.

Close up, the young woman appeared older than Karen had at first imagined, the exquisite make-up not quite obscuring a web of tiny strainlines around the lacquered mouth, and there was hardness in the demanding voice that repeated, 'Where is Mr Lammont?'

Not, Do you know? or Could you please tell me? but Where is he? and without even introducing herself.

Karen bridled, 'How should we know?' and Madeline glanced at her quickly, eyebrows raised.

The girl ignored Karen and addressed Madeline. 'Mr Lammont from the next cabin. You'll have seen him—tall and dark, and he'll probably have a fair-headed boy with him.'

Madeline was watching Karen. 'Leon,' she murmured.

'That's right.'

The girl's hard eyes ranged from Madeline to Karen, letting her gaze travel over the bare feet in their gold-strapped thongs, the white shorts, see-through cotton blouse, the hair tied little-girl style either side of her face. She took it all in, her eyes scornful.

'If you have any idea where they are you'd better tell me.'

Madeline spoke quietly. 'Had we? Mr Lammont appears to be a very private person. He didn't leave any instructions that he expected visitors.'

The woman compressed her lips. She made no effort to hide impatience, scarlet mouth drooped, her chin tilted in an attitude of challenge.

'I'm far from being a visitor.' She pronounced each word disdainfully.

'Oh. Are you?'

'Yes. I'm Leon's mother.'

On her left hand she wore a wide gold wedding ring, and now there was a hollow place where Karen's dreams had been. Leon's mother. Dain hadn't actually stated that he was separated from his wife; Karen had taken it for granted, and that had been foolish. If Dain had a son then very likely there would be a wife around somewhere. Of course there would.

Karen dropped her hands hastily on to her lap and

locked her fingers to prevent them shaking.

Madeline said coolly, 'I doubt whether anybody can tell you where Mr Lammont is, if he's not in his cabin. He moves about a lot. That's right, isn't it, Karen?'

Karen touched her dry lips with her tongue. I know where he is, her heart was shrieking ... He's in his rotten hideaway on his rotten island, and you're welcome to him ... but her dry lips could manage only, 'That's right.'

The girl regarded them suspiciously. She wasn't convinced. She stared at Karen's telltale twisted fingers, her expression insolent.

'Somebody must know,' she snapped. 'He must be somewhere around.'

Madeline kept her cool. 'Perhaps they can help you at the office. Why don't you ask?' and the girl in turquoise countered tersely, 'I've already done that. Naturally. As soon as I discovered him missing.'

'How disappointing for you.'

The girl tapped one foot restlessly on the edge of the patio, her eyes snapping.

'Blast him! So what do I do now?'

She wasn't really asking anybody, but Madeline offered, 'Perhaps you'd like a cup of tea. Or a cool drink.'

'No.' But the girl must have found Madeline's unruffled poise a little quelling, because she added reluctantly, 'No, thank you.'

She was so sure of herself. She glared at them as if they might have been personally responsible for Dain's absence, before she ordered, 'If he does arrive, you can tell him I was here. I'll be at the resort, and I expect him to collect me there.'

Madeline said softly, 'The resort is a large place.'

The girl tossed her head with its crown of short curls so like Leon's. 'I'll probably be in one of the bars. He can find me.'

She flounced away, high heels clicking on the path, well aware of the striking figure she made as she moved away, swaying her hips and shoulders, the gold wedding ring glinting on her finger.

'He'll just have to look for me,' the clear voice floated back to Madeline and Karen.

Madeline whispered, 'Well, well. What do you know? Who would have thought it?' but Karen wasn't capable of saying anything.

She was learning, though. She didn't flinch as Madeline added tartly, 'He won't have any trouble finding her if he does turn up. That one would stand out in any crowd, like a shark in a school of dolphin.'

Perhaps Madeline was pleased that Dain had disgraced himself by not admitting he had a wife, because she waited a moment, then she said pleasantly, 'Wasn't it splendid of Victor to take those extra days' leave to be with me? I think he must have expected my doctor's report to be depressing.'

'Will he stay in the other cabin with Andrew?'

'Possibly.' Madeline's eyes twinkled. 'He thought of staying with his friends, but Andrew could hardly refuse to share the cabin while he has it, could he? That would be inhospitable.'

Karen said gently, 'I'm glad Victor's here. You enjoy his visits, don't you?' hoping desperately that Madeline wouldn't ask whether Karen enjoyed Victor's visits as well. But Madeline sat quietly and after a while she said, 'My head is nodding. I might lie down for half an hour or so. No, don't fuss, child.' She put a hand on Karen's shoulder, pushing her down into her chair. 'Stay here and relax. I'm full of joy and relief, and I'm beautifully sleepy, that's all.'

Dispirited, Karen closed her own eyes. Listen to the birds, she told herself. Breathe deep and take the flower fragrance into your lungs; anything to hold at bay the dreadful knowledge that she had been an ass again, creating fantasies out of casual encounters.

She shut her eyes tighter and heard her heart beating, and someone came striding down the path and it couldn't be Dain because he was out on his island, and yet it was so like his long firm strides, the sound growing stronger as whoever was walking drew closer, and she thought, I won't open my eyes, but her eyes had a will of their own and they opened, and there he was, looking down at her. Dain Lammont.

She heard her voice ask, 'What are you doing here?' He sat in the chair Madeline had vacated, and frowned at her.

'You said you were taking Leon back to your island.'

'So I did, and thanks for the welcome.' Was it really only this morning they had walked over the dunes and he had said, 'You've had a lucky escape', and she had known there had been no escape at all, only a rapture of the senses that had trapped her into yet another dilemma.

Dain was speaking, and his voice came from a long way off, although he sat so near she felt his every movement.

'When I got back to the boat, Leon was in a tizzy. The tide brought in a shoal of whiting and he was so excited he couldn't keep still. We had to do some more fishing. I've re-stocked the larder and there's some for you, if you want it.'

No, thank you. It would choke me ... That was what she wanted to answer.

Instead she gulped and stammered, 'Your wife is here. She came on the midday plane. She's looking for you,' and hated herself for the betraying quiver in her voice.

'My wife.' His voice was very soft, almost silky. 'I
wonder who that could be?'

'You mean, you don't know?'

His lips relaxed in a faint half-smile, but he was
frowning, watching her, and the smile played only
around his mouth.

'How could I know, since I don't have a wife?' Now
the smile crept to his eyes. 'Not yet, that is,' his voice
even quieter, so soft she only just heard the words.
Was he trying to tell her something? Oh heaven, don't
let me get carried away again. She steeled herself
against the suggestion in his quizzical expression.

She blurted, 'The girl said—she's Leon's mother.
How do you explain that?'

'Oh—Carla!' He looked startled, and not altogether
delighted. 'What the devil is she doing here?'

'Maybe you'd better ask her. She left a message to
say you'll find her at the resort, in one of the bars.'

'That figures.'

Karen said defensively, 'We did offer her a drink.
We weren't entirely inhospitable,' and his mouth
quirked again.

'I'm sure you weren't. I can vouch for that.' He
added softly, 'Carla was my brother's wife. Now his—
widow.' He paused before the word, as though it might
have rankled.

Karen confessed naïvely, 'I thought Leon was your
son,' and he looked startled again, eyebrows flying so
that the creases vanished and a hint of amusement
lurked deep in the jetblack eyes.

'Did you now? That just shows, doesn't it, that you
may not be half as smart as you think.' Then he
sobered, grimness in his voice. 'Leon is my nephew,
my bother's only child. Dieron, Leon's father, died
several years ago.' He became remote then, as if he
had no more explanations to offer, pulling shutters

down over his feelings. Then he stood abruptly.

'I'd better find Carla before I go back to Leon. He's happy for the moment, cleaning his second batch of fish. It seems we shan't get back to Blunteree tonight. Did you——?'

He sent a silent question at Karen, and she shook her head. 'I didn't tell her about your island, if that's what you're wondering. What about your work, will it have to wait longer?'

She wished he didn't have that hint of weariness in the way he straightened his back, tightened his jaw. It stirred her maternal instincts. Or were they maternal, the impulses that made her want to reach out and grasp his hand, to make some small gesture to show him she understood all the frustration?

But she watched silently as he walked away, and later when he returned Karen was thankful she hadn't yielded to that impulse. Because the girl, Carla, came with him, clinging possessively to his arm, talking loudly, excitedly, with her upturned face lifted to his as she walked, so that he had to guide her to make sure those foolish shoes with their stiletto heels didn't cause her to stumble.

He did it patiently, listening gravely as she talked, and as they passed Madeline commented, 'My! They make a striking pair, don't they?'

Karen had to admit they did, indeed.

That evening, she and Madeline and Victor went to the kiosk restaurant for dinner, because Victor wanted to celebrate Madeline's good news. Karen wore her green dress, and brushed her hair so that it hung straight to her shoulders, light and springy, and Victor said, blushing slightly, 'Your hair is magic tonight, Karen. Sprinkled with gold dust, I think.'

His admiration was a confidence-booster and she had another as they entered the restaurant, because the four boys who had brought Red Emperor fish stood up from their table and clustered around her, vying for her attention.

She was pulling herself free when a small hand clutched her elbow, and she spun around to find Leon laughing a welcome. He told her about the fish, flashing fingers telling her size and number, indicating he wished she had been there.

Karen firmly refused to look around her. Leon was dressed in crisp shirt and shorts, and she suspected he and Dain must be eating here, and Carla too, so very soon she would have to wave and smile and look happy to see them.

Suppose their tables were close? How could she bear it?

Leon pointed to a secluded table in one corner, and Karen produced a polite smile, a light wave. Carla raised a languid hand, but Dain, grim-faced and reticent, face stern in soft red candlelight, simply lifted those flying brows and gave her a whimsical look before he rose to greet Madeline and Victor.

Madeline, refusing to be intimidated by anybody, held a short animated conversation with Dain, despite Carla's obvious lack of interest; and came back looking smug because she had unearthed news.

'He isn't married,' she hissed. 'He introduced that minx as his sister-in-law,' and Victor hushed her.

'You don't know she's a minx,' he reproved; but he added, 'I've never seen you so pleased with yourself, Aunt Madie. We should have brought champagne. You'd be flying higher than a kite after the first glass!'

'I don't need it. I'm high on good news and gratitude to whatever fates there be, because I'm a whole woman again.'

Karen would have preferred to sit where she could ignore that other table in the corner, but Victor drew out a chair for her, where she could see Dain and Carla clearly, and she had trouble all through the meal keeping her attention away from them.

Although Carla was not Dain's wife she looked very possessive, and Dain didn't appear discouraging. On the contrary, he was devoting all his attention, being exceedingly pleasant, and neither of them paid much heed to Leon, who tried to divert Karen several times, and even wandered across to her table until firmly brought back to his seat by Carla.

Carla didn't, Karen noticed, appear too motherly, but then she was obviously not the maternal type.

They were near enough for Karen to hear often the metallic tinkle of her laughter, but Dain kept his voice low, confidential, and Karen felt shut out.

Afterwards, in Madeline's cabin as they sat playing one of Victor's card games, Karen was only too well aware of lights in Dain's place, shining yellow through the trees. Long after Victor had left, the lights still glowed, and they were still bright when Madeline and Karen retired for the night.

Somewhere a radio played and the music drifted sweetly through the gardens, almost moving her to tears, she felt so dispirited.

Except that somewhere, deep in her heart, the small voice of hope dared suggest that perhaps Dain might be a reluctant host. After all, he couldn't send Leon's mother away, or could he?

Next morning there were faint shadows around Karen's eyes. She disguised them with make-up, so that no one could guess she had spent the night wakeful and lonely because Dain Lammont had come to his cabin with a smart young woman clinging to his arm.

She decided savagely that Dain must be used to sharing his quarters with females. She was hurt and needed to lash out at somebody, and when Dain and Leon set off for the beach later that morning, she fumed at herself for noticing their departure, and for caring.

After Dain and Leon went away, Carla came to Madeline's cabin to ask the time because, she confessed prettily, her watch had stopped. Karen suspected this was a pretext; after all, she had a radio in her cabin. But they were sitting outside and there seemed no reason why Carla couldn't join them.

She was in a different mood this morning, no longer alooof, but composedly friendly.

Karen was packing Madeline's needlework in tissue paper, sorting it into boxes, and Carla deigned to admire.

Karen wanted to scream, 'Don't touch it!' With a shock, she realised she was inexcusably jealous, and shook herself out of it as she went inside to collect drinks and biscuits. And if she allowed herself to say inwardly 'I hope it chokes you,' she felt that was allowable because it couldn't harm anybody.

Carla wore a scanty dark-blue crochet bikini, with a brightly coloured hippie-band across her forehead, blonde curls tumbled like Leon's, and every inch of her was perfect and dramatic.

When Karen came outside, she had taken possession of her chair, stretching out with eye-catching grace, and she accepted the glass Karen offered with a, 'Put it on the table, dear,' as if Karen were a waitress.

She reached out for the glass, swallowing its contents in one long gulp.

'I'll have another. I'm just dying of thirst.'

Yes, Carla was definitely dramatic, and deplorably bad-mannered, Karen decided, pouring another glass, which Carla accepted without a thank-you, as she said, 'Tell me, how did you feel when you discovered yourself holidaying next door to such a devastating person as Dain?'

Karen didn't answer because she didn't believe Carla expected any reply, and she was right.

Carla had a bombshell to drop, and she intended to drop it with maximum impact. She put down her glass with a thump, so that some of its contents spilled over on to one piece of Madeline's embroidery, before she licked her scarlet mouth so that it gleamed, and announced clearly, 'When we're married, I expect I shall have to keep brushing off all those clinging females Dain attracts.' The red lips shaped themselves into a dazzling smile, directed at Madeline. 'He does attract them, you know—all the impressionable girls. Birds, he calls them. Chicks. Always laughing. He gets a ton of amusement out of his fan clubs, as we call them. He seems to pick up adorers wherever he goes.'

She retrieved her glass, this time sipping slowly.

'Of course, I'll have to put my foot down after we're married. It would get terribly tedious, wouldn't it, eternally having to defuse all those passionate poor silly little things who get crushes on him.'

Karen managed to say tartly, 'Perhaps you overestimate his charm. He doesn't do anything for me,' and Carla wriggled disbelieving eyebrows and gave her tinkling laugh, while Madeline rescued her cushion cover from Carla's spillage. Her voice was only mildly interested.

'You and Dain plan to marry, do you? How soon?'

'Soon as possible.' Again the artificial laugh. 'My last marriage was a mistake. I married a weak man. Poor Dieron had no backbone at all. But this time I'll marry for strength. No one can say I didn't learn from my mistake.'

Madeline stroked her jaw thoughtfully.

'Soon as possible—does that mean *very* soon?'

Karen looked at Madeline quickly. That seemed an odd sort of question, as if she were really interested;

but Carla answered promptly, 'It certainly does,' and Madeline asked no more questions.

Carla continued, 'We'll fly back to the mainland on tomrrow's plane, Dain and Leon and myself. There's a lot to do.' She waved her hands gracefully. 'Special licence to arrange, and of course a new school for Leon.'

Karen heard a voice that didn't sound much like her own say, 'Dain didn't say he was going to be married,' and that seemed to startle Carla a little, although she recovered quickly.

'It's not exactly official yet. We thought it better, in view of the circumstances——'

Carla glanced down at her hands, where several rings sparkled on the slender fingers of both hands. 'It's time to tie up loose ends now, to get ourselves settled. It's practical, too. Dain simply adores Leon, but he can't look after the boy on his own. Dain's such a gipsy, he had to get the wanderlust out of his system first. I understood that, of course.'

I understand Dain perfectly, she was implying. She preened herself, patting her curls with beautifully manicured fingers.

'Like most men,' she cooed, 'Dain just needed the right woman to make up his mind for him, to point him in the proper direction.' She looked so pleased with herself. 'So I did it. I'm a great little organiser.'

I'll bet you are, Karen reflected bitterly, watching Carla stretch out her legs before she stood up in one lithe movement. Its studied effect was not lost on Karen. Carla was very poised, very attractive—and very wordly. Just like your boy-friend, she added silently, not without pain.

'We'll expect new neighbours, then.'

Madeline wasn't entirely regretful; she liked to see people come and go.

'I don't know. Dain might keep the cabin on for a bit, in case we want to spend the occasional few days.'

'Or your honeymoon.' Karen almost said it aloud, she was so angry. Such a beautiful place for a honeymoon, that cabin among secluded gardens, with the golden shower trees and the hibiscus, with flower-fragrance sweetening every breath of air.

Carla glided away towards her own cabin, then poised between garden and path she said carelessly, 'Thanks for the refreshment. Sorry I have to leave, but there's a lot to do. I mustn't forget I have a wedding to arrange.'

Madeline's expression was innocent, but her eyes inspected Karen with curiosity and with caring.

As Carla moved away she said softly, 'Your options are being whittled down, Karen. I hope you didn't care too much for either of the defaulting gentlemen.'

'You're not labelling Dain a defaulter, I hope?' Karen didn't feel her smile was a great success. 'Dain was never interested in me,' she confessed. 'He was just—whiling away the time.'

'Did you send Andrew packing while I was at Rockhampton, or shouldn't I ask? I wondered why he isn't around.'

'Why shouldn't you ask?' Karen swallowed. 'We had—a few words. A disagreement. I didn't see him after that. He could be spending time with his friends at the resort.' She stood up abruptly. 'I'd better see if there's any mail, and collect what we need from the store.'

There were no letters for her, several for Madeline. Karen avoided looking at the rest of the mail. If there was any correspondence in the rack for the perfidious Dain Lammont, or whatever he called himself this week, she didn't want to know about it.

Dain and Leon were away most of the day, and

Karen found her disobedient and treacherous thoughts escaping her control and swinging his way more often than she liked to admit.

She railed against him, calling him hard names in her heart, yet being honest enough to know that never, never once had he led her to believe that he offered more than casual friendship.

Twice he had drawn back when the contact between them looked like flaring into something explosive. So there was no excuse for the burning resentment she felt because he planned to spend the rest of his life with Carla. He had made a choice. It was his privilege, wasn't it? His privilege, and her pain.

Certainly, when Dain returned towards evening with Leon, he showed no signs of being aware that he might have inflicted mortal hurt on anybody. He carried a box of papers into his cabin, and Leon followed with a portable typewriter. Leon had been told about his flight to Rockhampton next day, he made excited swooping motions, simulating flight, and that reminded Karen about the plastic kite.

She hoped it was safely stowed away in the hut on Blunteree. She couldn't bear to think of it drifting about on the clifftop for the wind to sweep away.

She beckoned to Leon, touched his pocket, and he pulled out the notebook and 'talking pen'. She took them and wrote 'Kite' with a big question mark. He giggled, drew a picture of the hut, and Karen nodded.

Leon crumpled the paper and dropped it in the bin, and for this she was grateful. She didn't want Dain finding out she had been concerned about a child's plaything, a simple plastic kite he had probably put together in ten minutes one day to keep Leon entertained while he worked on his scripts.

Karen walked back to sit with Madeline in the shade, and Dain emerged from his cabin, hair tumbled over his forehead, face taut under the tan.

'Move over, Golden Hair. I need a rest.'

Karen said wildly, 'You won't be able to call me that silly name after tomorrow. I'm dying it red—my hair, that is.'

'Good heavens, whatever for?'

He didn't believe her, and Madeline came to her rescue—'We females are addicted to change,'—so that his brows drew together as if he knew there were undercurrents but didn't quite understand which way they were running.

There were deepening lines on Dain's face and the haggard look had returned, but Karen hardened herself against sympathy. She was tired; she didn't want to talk to anybody, and Dain Lammont could take his strained and weary face to someone else for solace.

She certainly wasn't prepared for the arrival of both Victor and Andrew soon afterwards, although Madeline was delighted.

'We're having a garden party!' she exulted, gliding inside for more refreshments, while Leon collected extra chairs from Dain's cabin.

Andrew lounged against a banksia tree. He gave Karen an apologetic grin. For once he wasn't sure of himself. He explained how he and Victor had met on the beach, and he glanced sideways at Dain as if he might have feared Dain knew of his reckless telephone call to the police.

But Dain was being uncommunicative. Once he offered Karen a shadow-smile, and her heart turned over, but that was weakness, and she walked away to talk to Andrew.

Victor had been sailing with his friend, Les. 'One of the best, Les is,' he informed them warmly, 'He'll put up with me at his house as long as I can stay.'

Andrew would have to leave his cabin tomorrow,

and since Victor carefully avoided including Andrew in his plans, this was probably the last time Karen and Andrew would see each other. She hoped so.

However, she needed to show Dain she was unaffected by his desertion, and the only way to do it was to be pleasant to Andrew. She stayed close to him, hating herself but not flinching when he draped a casual arm over her shoulders.

As Madeline came out with another platter of biscuits and cheeses, Andrew announced, 'I'm leaving tomorrow. Have to, I'm afraid. I'm being turfed out.'

It was like a public announcement, and if he waited expectantly for someone to offer a bed so that he could stay longer, he waited in vain.

Madeline answered brightly, 'No doubt you have lots to do at home, with your wedding and everything,' and that put him back a little, but Karen could feel his fingers curving into the flesh on her shoulder, then he said clearly, 'I might persuade Karen to come up north for a while and have a look at Cairns.'

He was hesitant about it, but Karen said, 'I just might do that,' while nobody else spoke.

. . . I just might do that . . . It had been a silly thing to say; she'd blurted it out on the spur of the moment. A challenge, to throw before Dain, who was making arrangements for his future that didn't include her.

Victor looked faintly shocked, Madeline donned her headmistress-face, and even Andrew appeared startled.

But Karen didn't retract. Dain had to understand that he could go off and marry Carla, or anybody else he chose, and it would mean nothing to her because she had other plans. Never, never would he be allowed to guess that she had so far forgotten herself as to weave dreams around him.

Karen busied herself collecting empty glasses, and

when she looked at Dain and asked casually, 'Another drink?' he refused. He looked stern, his jaw set white-hard against tanned skin, and his eyes were flint-hard.

Karen fled inside. She clattered dishes, until Madeline came lightfooted, gentle-handed, behind her.

'Are you going to Cairns, Karen?' Her voice was soft so that no one outside would hear what she said.

Karen answered promptly, 'Of course not,' and Madeline sat down, watching silently, until after a few moments she said, 'I suppose you know what you're doing.'

Karen managed a crooked smile, and Madeline sighed. 'It's that Lammont person, isn't it?' Don't worry, he's gone.' She hesitated. 'I expect you'd guessed I was hoping you and Victor——' and Karen left the glasses and hugged her affectionately.

'That's a wonderful compliment, but I don't bring good luck to people I get fond of, and I'm going to be very careful not to get emotional about anybody in future. Let's not talk about me any more.'

'Can we discuss you for just one more minute?' Madeline's face glowed with feeling. 'If I'm allowed to ask, what are your plans when you leave me? I don't enquire just of curiosity. I have contacts in Queensland. If you're seeking another position, per-haps I could help.'

'That would be marvellous—truly marvellous!' So she wasn't without friends, after all. Her spirits lifted. She whispered, 'What do you fancy for dinner when Andrew leaves, or do we have to invite him?' and they were giggling like conspirators when Jenna knocked at the door, and Karen discovered she had another friend.

'I came to see what you're doing tomorrow. Miller's sending me out on a mission and I thought you might like to come. I have to collect an unidentified object from the beach on one of the islands.'

Madeline laughed.

'You mean spacemen; little green fellows from Mars?' and Jenna's healthy laugh filled the cabin.

'No such luck! This is a huge piece of bone, probably the jawbone of a whale or something like that, Miller expects. He wants it for his collection, and I promised to try and bring it back. He's on duty tomorrow.' Her merry face turned towards Karen. 'I need a helper. Thought you might like to oblige.' She looked a question at Madeline. 'We'd be back for late lunch.'

'Of course she'll go, won't you, Karen? Just what every girl needs, an adventure with leftover whale. Something to tell your folks when you get home.'

Karen hesitated. 'Unless Victor has something planned,' then she added impulsively, 'Perhaps Victor would like to go.'

Why hadn't she thought of it before? . . . Victor and Jenna. The quiet gentle man, and the confident outgoing girl. They would be good together.

Jenna accepted practically, 'If it's okay with Madeline, the three of us can go. I wouldn't mind an extra pair of hands. Miller says the bone is as long as the boat and it could be hard to balance. We'll have to do a bit of juggling. That is, if Victor doesn't object.'

Madeline pulled a shrewd face. She knew what Karen had in mind, and her smile was understanding.

She said, 'Why don't you ask him?' and Jenna smiled, 'I will.'

Andrew seemed rather put out when he discovered he wasn't invited. Fortunately, his plane left in the middle of the day, and he dared not risk missing the flight. In any case, the boat was too small for an extra passenger.

Karen managed to manoeuvre herself a little while alone with him before Andrew left. She owed him that much. After all, she had encouraged him this afternoon while Dain listened, so it seemed only reasonable that she should make it clear to him that this was their final goodbye.

In his own shallow way he had cared, he still cared.

He wasn't pleased to find that behind her friendly manner Karen had erected a barrier that he could not pass any more. No blandishments, no persuasions, would develop their friendship any further.

They stood alongside a coral tree, its red clusters of bright flowers brushing his shoulders, and he squeezed Karen's fingers and urged, 'You still care about me, sweetheart, I know you do,' and Karen told him, 'You have one girl to care about now, Andrew, the girl you're going to marry.'

'Sweetheart', he had called her. The name that sounded so airy on Miller's lips had jarred.

She added, 'If I hadn't come to Australia, you would have forgotten about me already.'

He wore his little-boy-sulking expression, and Karen was amazed to find how easy it was to say her final goodbye.

She watched him walk away until he disappeared along the foreshore, and he did not look back. Part of her youth and innocence went with him. She would never be so trusting again, so naïve and foolish; so perhaps she should be grateful for the experience.

If Madeline found her another position she would come out of the whole incident with some scars, some grief, and a heap of knowledge that might prove invaluable in future.

Karen strolled back to the cabin where Madeline and Victor still sat under the green-roofed patio, and sunlight filtered on to the faces of those two people she knew would always be dear to her.

Tomorrow she would try persuading Victor to look at Jenna with eyes that really saw, appreciating the gay and vibrant girl instead of taking her for granted as he seemed to do.

Madeline and Victor stopped talking as she came back, both welcoming, both caring. They had guessed it would be a difficult goodbye for her, although Madeline would be surprised to know it had proved much easier than she expected.

Victor poured a drink, shook the bottle, pushed the glass towards her.

'Thank you.' Karen looked from one to the other. 'I've been saying goodbye to Andrew. I shan't have time to see him tomorrow. And thank you for the drink.'

Victor pushed a chair towards her, made her sit down, although it was past time to get the evening meal ready. He smiled at her over the rim of the glass he lifted to his lips.

'Anything for a friend,' he said.

CHAPTER TEN

THE sea next morning stayed mirror-flat, and Jenna said, 'Hooray for us! The fates must be on our side.'

She had the boat ready to catch the tide rising, so they would reach their objective at high tide and let the sea carry them as close as possible to the bone they wanted to pick up.

Jenna in her amethyst bikini was really something to look at. Skin deep-tanned, glossy black hair caught back in a long ponytail with a silver clasp, she organised the expedition with skill and confidence.

Karen wore her white shorts and yellow T-shirt and at Madeline's insistence a floppy sunhat. Karen had made a last-minute effort to induce Victor to go with Jenna alone, but Madeline would have none of it.

'You haven't much longer on the island. Go and have your adventure while I finish off my last bit of embroidery and stow it all away in a cupboard and forget it.'

Victor grinned. 'Aunt Madie, you have another week here at least. Idle fingers don't suit you. You can't possibly sit unemployed.'

'I have to,' she explained simply. 'As soon as this piece is finished, away it all goes. It's a symbolic gesture.'

Still Karen hovered. 'Shouldn't I stay with you, if that's going to be your final masterpiece?'

'No, Karen, you should not.' Madeline snipped off a length of bright purple thread. 'Off with you both. I need to be alone with my thoughts.'

She meant it. There were adjustments to be made, the slow sweet recognition of the fact that she could now begin again to make the plans abandoned when she became ill.

So Karen sat in the bows of the aluminium boat, Victor amidships, and Jenna handled the outboard motor from the stern, dashing over the water like Miller did, full speed, spreading plumes of white wash tumbling behind them.

When they came in sight of the small beach where Miller had directed them Jenna approached cautiously, edging around a headland to the gravelly beach, if you could call it a beach. It caught the wild winds from eastward, and although Miller's strange object straddled the high tide mark, there was plenty of evidence around it to suggest this beach took many a pounding.

Old and white and scarred, the bone lay among a heap of flotsam.

Karen gasped, 'What size whale would have a jaw-bone that size?' and Jenna laughed.

'Darned if I know, but it wasn't any sardine, that's for sure!'

'Is that the biggest bone you've ever seen?'

'Not the very largest, but it's well up there among the heftiest bits and pieces it's been my joy to discover.'

Jenna began pulling the boat over the gravel and Victor said quickly, 'I'll do that.'

Jenna had always liked Victor. She cheerfully allowed him to tug the boat clear of the water while she straddled the huge bone, planning ways of balancing it in the dinghy.

Karen stood beside her. 'Do we search for other parts of the whale?' and Jenna said, laughing, 'You can if you want to, but I doubt whether you'll find anything—bones, that is. You won't find unbroken shells here, either, it's too rugged. I'll take you shell-hunting before you leave, on one of the other beaches.'

Victor had pushed the dinghy under the heaviest part of the bone and Jenna said, 'That's fine. We'll make a boatman out of you yet,' and Victor confessed, 'I used to fantasise about that once—owning a yacht. Quite ridiculous, for a man who knows nothing about the sea.' He grinned. 'I was visualising something a little larger than Miller's dinghy.' He grimaced then, making a wistful face. 'A pipe-dream, of course. For one thing, I don't see myself handling anything in a rough sea. So I decided I wouldn't try.'

'You can do anything you want to,' Jenna contradicted, frowning at him in disapproval. 'You shouldn't be so deplorably negative. If I were you, I'd go straight out and buy that yacht and learn how to use it. That's if your bank balance will let you,' she added. She reproached him across the arched white bone, her eyes flashing. 'Anything you want to do, you can do, if you're prepared to learn,' she insisted, and Victor said Yes, he probably could, if you put it like that.

He was surveying Jenna as if he had never seen her before, boyish face under the grey hair faintly amused, but Karen noticed that from the moment Jenna challenged him, Victor lost most of his shyness.

He tucked into the awkward job of loading the curved bone into the boat, taking time to haggle, discuss and experiment, until finally it projected like the figurehead of a viking ship from the bow, balanced precariously.

And that was how they brought the great white bone back to Wapparaburra, travelling carefully, with Karen and Victor supporting the strange cargo. They received some odd looks and ironic cheers as they snaked between yachts and fishing boats, then among the jet-ski riders outside Miller's boatshed.

The unloading was a breeze compared with the trouble of loading. Jenna's mouth curved excitedly, but she only said, lightly, 'I hope Miller appreciates all we've been through to get this little toy for him.'

Karen touched the bone curiously.

'What will he do with it?'

'I don't know. Add it to his beachcombing collection, probably, or hang it over a doorway somewhere. He didn't say, but I'll bet he's got plans for it.'

Jenna hoisted the bone waist-high and Victor took it from her, putting his shoulder under the main weight, lowering it onto the sand.

'Wait until I can help you,' he ordered quietly, and Jenna pulled a little face and said, "Yes, Sir," but she left the heaviest part of the load to Victor, and they pulled the bone halfway up the beach between them before Victor came back to collect the motor.

Victor uncoupled the motor while Karen cleaned the boat and Jenna took the oars out of the rowlocks.

Victor had enjoyed himself this morning; he seemed younger, freer, more sure of himself.

He smiled at Karen, a carefree smile that set his eyes glinting, then the smile widened and deepened and Karen saw that he looked over her shoulder to where Jenna stood, brushing sand from between her toes.

They were exchanging glances, Jenna and Victor, communicating in the way people use when they no longer have a need for words. Jenna's lips smiled secretly as she picked up the oars and carried them to the boatshed and then stood waiting beside the bone as she had been bidden, while Victor stowed the motor and then joined her.

Karen saw the two figures in the distance and as they reached the edge of the bushland they stopped, arguing apparently, then each took one end of the giant bone and they staggered on with it. So something special could be happening between them.

Karen washed the last of the sand from the boat, thinking Well, now you've done it . . . as a matchmaker, you look like being a great success.

Her brief fling at being sought after was over . . . She had swung full circle back to unassuming Karen Fallon who didn't expect to stir any man to distraction.

The only difference was that now she had finally lost her wide-eyed dreams. There was a hollow feeling around her heart as she hurried to Madeline.

Madeline leaned back on her comfortable chair with her eyes closed, but as Karen arrived she stirred.

'I'm not asleep. I'm listening to every footstep on

the path and I recognised yours. Haven't missed a passer-by all morning. I've inspected all new arrivals and said farewell to the old. That nice young honeymoon couple left. And Carla and Leon. Leon went off in great style, riding on Dain's shoulders. I never saw a child enjoy things more than that boy.'

Yes, Leon would have enjoyed that: riding on Dain's strong shoulders to wherever he was going. Karen imagined the three of them, Dain and Leon and Carla, laughing in the sunshine.

She let out her breath in a long sigh. 'So now they've all gone,' she mused aloud, and Madeline glanced at her shrewdly before she said, 'Not all. I don't know where Dain is now, but he didn't leave on the plane. He's certainly not with that hussy.'

'You mean Carla?'

'That I do,' Madeline nodded. 'She must have taken Leon with her. The three of them went to the airstrip, but he——' she flourished a casual hand in the direction of Dain's cabin—— 'he came back alone. Don't know where he's gone; he disappeared quick-smart once he arrived back here. Took his boxes and his typewriter, and off he went towards the beach somewhere.'

Somewhere in her heart Karen felt a rebirth of hope, but she managed to say steadily, 'Never mind about Dain. It's time for your extremely late lunch. Would you like a drink first?'

'No, thanks. I've soaked up my share of liquid refreshment this morning.' Madeline followed Karen inside. 'Tell me about the trophy. Was it the remains of a spaceman?'

'No, everything was very terrestrial. It's the jawbone of a large whale, Jenna says.'

'And Victor?' Madeline's expression was carefully innocent. 'What have you done with him? Not fed him to the surviving whales, I hope, or marooned him on the beach. Did you bring him back with you?'

'He's helping Jenna.' Karen flushed. She felt a little guilty, not altogether sure how Madeline regarded her matchmaking; but the older woman smiled back with understanding.

'Helping Jenna, is he? Well, if I can't have you for my favourite nephew, I expect Jenna will do very well. Although it's early days yet, isn't it?'

Yes, it was early days yet. But there had been something especially caring in Victor's manner as he took the heavy load from Jenna, a new confidence. Perhaps it was a promise.

Madeline had completed her work, and after lunch Karen finished packing it all away. Boxes of achievement, every one representing so much time, so much patience.

Then she wrote letters while Madeline rested. She didn't find much to say in her letters. She tried to be lighthearted, especially in the card to her mother. 'This morning we collected a U.F.O. which turned out to be whalebone. We had terrific fun' . . . but most of what she wanted to say was left out. I don't know where I'll be two weeks from now, or what I'll be doing, but don't you worry about it. I'll do all the worrying. That was what she could have added. . . . I have to leave this fantastic island and maybe I shall come home, since I don't see any positive future ahead of me.

She didn't mention Andrew. Not to her mother. Not to her girl friends in Canada. There had been a card from Linda and Melanie, forwarded airmail by her mother without comment. Karen knew her mother would have felt a lot better if she, Karen, were sending postcards from Canada.

She sighed and signed the last letter. Victor had disappeared after lunch, presumably to help Jenna again with the whalebone. He joined Madeline and Karen for an evening meal, then Jenna slipped in quietly to join them, and Miller came down to register his thanks for the souvenir.

They walked together through the valley to the beach, Jenna and Victor walking ahead, Miller whistling a teasing love song, while Jenna blushed; and Karen mused, It's so obvious, so quickly . . . and tried to imagine if the way she had felt about Dain when he brought her back from the island had shown so clearly. Perhaps it had.

It was dusk when they walked back, lights shone in most of the cabin windows, rectangles of gold turning the trees into black lace. But the cabin next door to Madeline's remained shrouded in shadows. Wherever he was, Dain was leaving his place for the possums and nightbirds to haunt, while he occupied some other position where no one could reach him. No one, Karen mused. Could that be it? That he needed nobody.

It was odd, how confident Carla had been, how adamant that Dain was taking her today to arrange that special wedding licence. She could have been lying, of course. As Karen undressed for sleep she came back to that thought. People sometimes did lie, deliberately, callously, for reasons of their own. Some kinds of people.

Karen knew Carla disliked her. Could she have been issuing some kind of warning? And if she lied about this one point, wasn't it possible she lied about other things as well? Like 'This time I'm marrying for strength'.

Dain had never mentioned marriage to Carla, never in his conversations here or on his own island.

Next morning Karen arose pleasantly lighthearted, because some time in the night she had come to a decision. She would talk to Dain next time he came to sit in the shade of their patio. *If* he came to sit with them.

It wasn't going to do much for her ego if she asked him forthrightly whether he intended marrying Carla and he replied, 'Of course I am, and what is it to you?' but that was a risk she would have to take. After all, Karen reminded herself wryly, there wasn't all that much left of her pride.

She could ask Dain about his plans for the future, keeping it light, asking friendly questions so that he would never guess the importance of his answers.

She dressed casually in a flowered sundress; she shampooed her hair and brushed it, before she got on with her chores. But Dain's cabin remained locked and silent.

After lunch Madeline said, 'Victor wants to take me to meet his friends, the man with the yacht and his family. Will you come with us?' and it seemed to Karen that a way was being made for her.

She asked, 'Do you need me?' and Madeline replied, 'No, I don't need you, but I'd be delighted to have you along, and so would Victor and his friends.'

Like pieces of jigsaw, put in place by invisible hands, the pattern of what she must do appeared to Karen.

'If you don't mind, I do have something I should see to when I get a chance. I could do it while you and Victor go visiting.'

'That might be a good idea.' Madeline gave no indication of whether she suspected Karen might be going in search of Dain, and when she and Victor had departed on their visiting, Karen clutched the floppy sunhat and ran for Miller, praying he would be near his boatshed.

He was in the kiosk gardens, walking around his new souvenir, admiring the great arch of bone.

Karen gasped, 'Miller, is your boat available, please?' and he grinned.

'Sweetheart, you're lucky. It's all set up—motor, oars, the lot. Took a young bloke out fishing this

morning and haven't had time to put anything away
yet.'

'Miller, you're wonderful!'

Karen wanted to throw her arms around him, to hug
him, to kiss him, out of her overwhelming gratitude.
He went to the boatshed with her to check the fuel
tank, and soon she was on the water.

She steered straight out across the channel, taking a
wide sweep towards Blunteree, because everything had
fallen into place and she wanted to arrive as fast as she
could.

Sun dancing on water, wind trying to blow the
floppy sunhat off her head, she went directly for Dain's
island, not letting herself ponder about what kind of
reception she would get or whether she would have to
crawl back to Wapparaburra, rejected. Andrew had
taught her to accept that sort of situation; it wouldn't
kill her.

Blunteree shone in the sun, a green umbrella on blue
water, rocky coastline formidable but the one small
beach shining as light hit the quartz pebbles.

Karen went in slowly and as she crossed the reef
that now showed clear underwater she looked up, and
there, wraithlike in the sky, floated the bird shape of
Leon's kite.

She followed it for one incredulous moment before
she had to concentrate in the shallows, choosing her
way between dark underwater canyons and projecting
coral.

She beached Miller's boat and searched the sky
again, but the kite had vanished from sight.

She pulled the dinghy to safety and scrambled up
the cliff-face, remembering Madeline saying that Dain
had left Carla and Leon at the airstrip and come back
alone. Perhaps she had been mistaken. It wasn't important, anyway.

What mattered was that someone was on the island, and she found herself running, running, along the rim of the saucer-dip, then plunging into the groves of trees, as if the happiness of her whole future life depended on her finding Dain. And perhaps it did.

When she stumbled out of the last casuarinas on to the slope on the other side of the island, she saw the straight-backed figure of the kite-flyer. Not Leon, but Dain.

He wore the scruffy denim jeans, rolled-up cuffs, and a fierce blue shirt that must have been unbuttoned because it flapped in the light wind as he sat there, hands taut on the kite-string.

Now that she had actually arrived, that she was near enough to see the sinews in the strong brown neck, dark hair flopping as the breeze stirred it, Karen found herself almost turning back, so great was her over-whelming shyness.

So here I go, asking for another setback, she was telling herself, when the man half-turned as though he sensed that he was not alone.

He stiffened, then, shoulders rigid, head flung back, and Karen's heart took a plunging dive before she summoned her defences and walked slowly towards him across the grass. He squinted up along the kite-string, unwinding so the kite rose higher, before he said, without looking at her, 'Don't sit down, unless you're here to stay.'

'Wh-What sort of welcome is that?' Was that her own voice, coming out with the quavering hesitation of an intimidated child? He turned and measured her with his clever eyes, saying nothing, but putting out one brown hand and patting the dry grass beside him.

Karen sat down carefully, arranging herself so that no part of her body brushed against his. And for all her carefulness, the feeling between them could not have been stronger if they had actually made contact.

A tingling set all her senses vibrantly aware, as though he touched her. She could not have been more conscious of him if he had reached out his arms and pulled her towards him.

'Why did you come, Golden Hair?'

Karen gathered all her courage and asked huskily, 'Is it true? Are you going to marry Carla?'

'Wherever did you get that idea?'

'I just—wondered.'

He said grimly, 'Carla is the last woman I'd be likely to marry.'

Karen blinked at the frothy ocean below, not letting him see the relief in her eyes.

'I don't suppose you'd like to tell me why?'

The breeze stirred a few strands of Karen's hair and when they brushed his shoulder Dain took one hand from the kite-string and smoothed the blowing strands back in place, and his touch was like a lighted fuse, travelling along her skin, kindling flames.

He said, 'My brother Dieron was a sensitive man, a dreamer. He wasn't cut out for working on the land, yet fate somehow organised his life so he finished up working that way. Like a lot of pleasant people, he wasn't strong enough to push against outside pressures. Being the elder, he was destined to take over our family property in the far west of New South Wales. I inherited a smaller property and put in a manager straight away.

'Poor Dieron, he wasn't keen about tending sheep. And I settled for another kind of life; my kind. Selfish, I suppose, or just plain thoughtless.'

He stirred restlessly. 'If only he'd told me how he hated it! If he'd given some of us—his family—a clue, we surely could have worked out something between us. Anyhow, he didn't. He just went along with things.

Then our parents died, killed together in a car smash.

'Dieron married Carla and took over management of the property. Leon was born, unfortunately deaf. Then came the drought, three hellish years of it. Dieron was too sensitive to yell for help, or perhaps he didn't comprehend exactly how far things had deteriorated. Maybe he was the eternal optimist. Anyway, he lost everything.

'And one day, when the drought finally broke, by some terrible irony of fate he drowned in a flooded creek, trying to save some weakened animal. The property is Carla's now—worthless, of course, without money to re-stock it.'

'But Leon—you said he was neglected.'

'I probably should have used the world "unloved". He wasn't physically neglected, just left to the tender mercies of a careless governess. He's been taught sign language, but I believe he has tremendous potential.

'There's a lot more he should learn. In appearance he's like his mother, but there's a great deal of Dieron in him. At the moment he's high-spirited, basking in attention; but he's extremely sensitive. Carla hankers for the life of a social butterfly. What little money there is left of Dieron's, she spends on clothes and cars and fancy entertainment. Leon needs somebody to love and understand him.'

His voice, usually so composed, shook a little. 'That's a lot to ask of a woman, isn't it? Will you please love and understand me, and by the way, would you mind taking on my nephew as well, plus any children we may have together?'

Karen said cautiously, 'That would depend on the woman you're asking, don't you think?'

A faint smile touched his mouth, as if she might have answered him more truly than she knew; as if there might have been some kind of promise implicit in her quiet rejoinder.

He began winding in the kite-string. Karen settled herself more comfortably beside him.

'Is Leon here, or did he go in the plane?'

'He went to the mainland with his mother, but he'll be back.' His voice was bleak. 'I drive a hard bargain.'

When Karen said nothing he went on, 'Guardianship of my brother's boy in return for a guarantee that dear Carla will continue to live the gay life for which she hankers.'

He sounded unbelievably cynical; Karen decided she couldn't blame him.

The radiant boy who might have remained confined to an isolated property that offered him every comfort but love; the death of a brother who had been made to feel inadequate, labelled a failure by a demanding wife; even his work among developing nations that must sometimes show him the crueller side of what human beings can do to each other. They would all contribute to his pain.

Yes, Dain was entitled to bitterness. She only wished he hadn't elected to use it as a barrier, a sealing-off of himself from all but physical contact with those who might have loved him.

He said, 'You haven't answered my question. Why did you come?'

'She said—Carla—that you wanted somebody to look after Leon.'

She sighed then, a thin thread of sound, and Dain looked at her sharply.

'Of course I do. Have you come to offer yourself for the job?'

'Yes. If you find me acceptable.'

Her voice was anguished, and he looked away before he began to bring in the kite more quickly.

'Did it occur to you——' strong brown hands moved Leon's piece of board that held the string,—'that I

might also require some loving——' he reeled more
slowly, carefully, as the kite swooped and dived—'and
caring?' His eyes were on the hovering kite, the frail
birdshape gradually coming nearer. '—for myself? Or
that I might also require—a resident mermaid?'

Through the transparent shape Karen saw the sky
like a patch of misty blue. Or was it that her eyes had
filled with tears?

Still he did not look directly at her. He stood up and
grasped the hovering kite, lowered it slowly to the
ground.

Karen pulled a blade of dry grass.

'You didn't ever say so. That—that you needed a
mermaid. You said——'

'No,' he admitted. 'Perhaps that was a bad oversight,
a sad piece of misjudgment. But to tell you the truth,'
he wound the last of the string around the board and
dropped it beside the kite, and faced her abruptly, 'I
didn't think you were quite ready for a passionate declaration. Sometimes I wondered, once or twice when
you let the feeling take you and clung to me as though
you really wanted——'

He turned away, staring out over the sea that shim-
mered green blue and soft opal below them, at the
white waves frothing on the rocks.

'What happened to Lover Boy?' he demanded, in a
change of mood. 'Don't tell me you let him get away
again.'

She said in a small voice, 'I sent him away. I only
encouraged him because she said—Carla said—that
you were going to marry her.'

His hands became still.

'Don't tell me you were consumed with jealousy!'

Karen's voice was very controlled. 'I'm not telling
you anything.'

He had an unfair advantage, towering over her like

that. She scrambled to her feet, and moved a few paces away.

He didn't try to stop her, but he said. 'Perhaps you ought to try telling me a few things. You might consider giving me some inkling about the way you feel, and why you took the trouble to come all the way out here today, after all that carry-on with Andrew yesterday. Proposing to chase him north when that was only a halfhearted invitation he issued. Or didn't you see through him all that clearly?'

Disappointment shook her, tears threatened. She whispered, 'Why do you say things like that?' and he let her see the pain in his eyes, his pain and his need of her.

'Because if I'm making a mistake, if I'm reading something into those beautiful golden eyes that isn't really there, then I think,' his lips twisted, his breathing heavy like that of a man who scales mountains. 'I think I'd be inclined to put myself down on those rocks down there, because I don't much fancy life without you, and that's the truth.'

'That makes two of us,' she dared to say it, because of what she heard in his voice, read in his eyes.

How could she ever have thought him impassive? She took one small step towards him. Only one, because that was all that was necessary.

Already he had covered the space between them and his arms came around her hungrily, so that she gasped for breath and pushed against his chest until he laughed, and eased his grip, but did not let her go.

'The kite——' His mouth was on her skin, kissing cheeks and delicate jawline, lips creating trails of sensation wherever they touched. 'You know why I flew the kite, Golden Hair? I was desperate. I told myself,

Maybe she'll see it floating up there and come and look for me. Then I asked myself, what kind of crazy idea is that? But I flew it, just the same. A silly, childish game . . .'

Eyes brilliant, like polished jet, he cupped her face tenderly in his hands, face soft with the love he had never been able to express until today.

'And then,' he added softly, 'then you came.'

Karen lifted both her arms and linked her fingers on the back of his strong brown neck, pulling his face down towards hers again, until she could see every line on the dark, clever face.

'Oh yes,' she promised, 'you can be sure of that. Whenever you want me, I'll come. Even if—if you don't want me—I'll come anyway.'

Dain laughed again, the strong joyous laugh of a lover sure of his love.

'I've a better idea,' he said. 'Don't ever go away.'

Karen nodded blissfully. 'All right, I shan't go away. Not ever.'

He pulled her close again to the warmth of his own body, wrapping his arms around her so that she felt the steady thudding of his heart against the wild fluttering of her own, until at last there seemed a fusion between them, a blending of their two strengths. As if she were seeing not only with her own eyes but with his as well, feeling with his feelings, their two sets of senses combining so the whole island seemed to come alive.

Every sound, every movement, every rustle, belonged to them, intensified because they experienced it together.

It couldn't be possible that she had ever considered Dain only a physical man; he smiled down at her now out of those deep dark eyes, letting her see the man he was, searching her own features for every revealing expression.

'A glorious day,' Karen thought, and then he kissed her, and there was no day at all. Only the powerful mouth exploring hers, arousing the wave of sensuous pleasure that blotted out everything but the man who was telling her his love in his touching.

When he finally let her go, sliding his arms around her hips, holding her a little away from him while he loved her with his eyes, she stood there obediently; and then she said, 'Can we go to your hut now?'

'Mmmm. If you especially want to.' He wound his long strong fingers in her hair, bent and kissed her lips.

She said, 'I want to put that kite away where it will never be lost. I want it to last for ever.'

He said, 'Oh, the kite.' Laughter made his face young. 'I was hoping you had something else in mind,' he teased.

'Certainly not!'

He asked lazily, 'You mean, I have to wait until we're married?' and she asked shyly, 'Are you planning to marry me?'

He kept one arm around her waist as he reached down to pick up kite and string.

'I am. Just as soon as it can be arranged. You just try and wriggle your way out of that, young lady!'

He arranged the kite under his free arm, keeping it in place with his elbow, and Karen remembered the folder of papers the day she had arrived at the airport, and Dain striding away grim-faced.

Now she traced the miraculous change in his laughing face, and marvelled. How far they had both come since then . . .

Hand in hand like children they walked away from the clifftop, towards the log hut. Above them a flock of seagulls wheeled, shattering silence with their cries, dipping and gliding before they plunged down to the water's edge. A purple velvet butterfly exercised its wings, slowly and gracefully, on a lantana flower; and a light wind made music in the casuarina trees . . . incredibly soothing . . . incredibly sweet.

Harlequin® Plus

A ROMANCE CLASSIC

When Madeline calls Dain a "Heathcliff of a man," she is not exactly giving him a compliment. For Heathcliff is the handsome, but strangely menacing hero of *Wuthering Heights,* a famous romantic novel by Emily Brontë published in England in 1848.

Wuthering Heights is the story of the beautiful Catherine Earnshaw and the orphaned Heathcliff, brought into the Earnshaw household as a child. As he grows up, Heathcliff is cruelly tormented by Hindley, Catherine's jealous and petty older brother. Catherine is Heathcliff's protector—and kindred spirit, because they share a love for the eerie desolate beauty of the lonely Yorkshire moors. Only Catherine can still the turbulent angry emotions that smolder behind the troubled Heathcliff's dark eyes.

Eventually Catherine marries a prosperous neighbor—an act Heathcliff cannot accept. He refuses to forgive her and accuses her of destroying him. After Catherine dies in childbirth, Heathcliff challenges her ghost to haunt him, crying, "Be with me always—take any form—drive me mad! Only do not leave me in this abyss where I cannot find you!"

So blinded is Heathcliff by his obsessive love and his feelings of betrayal that, like the Devil himself, he swears revenge and spends many years slowly and methodically destroying the lives of everyone around him. And, still haunted by Catherine, he begins to wander the moors, searching for her. He looks forward to his own death—to his deranged mind an hour of triumph—and when it comes, his spirit joins Catherine's, and they are united again at last.

Harlequin Romances

The books that let you escape
into the wonderful world of romance!
Trips to exotic places...interesting
plots...meeting memorable people...
the excitement of love....These are
integral parts of Harlequin Romances —
the heartwarming novels read by
women everywhere.

Many early issues are now available.
Choose from this great selection!

Choose from this list of
Harlequin Romance editions.*

Some of these book were originally published under different titles.